Spur

By

Ann Jenkerson

ISBN: 978-0-578-03541-3

To Sharon and Alan, A.C., and Carole

1

Tears streamed down Lisa's face as she called into the darkness, "Oh Grant, where are you when I need you!" She fumbled with the flashlight, trying to loosen the spare tire with the tire tool. She tried desperately to remember the steps to changing a tire. She had watched Grant do it a dozen times, although not with enough attention to remember every detail. The hazard lights were on and a flare that she had found in the back of the mini-van glowed at the side of the highway. Two cars had passed in the night, despite the fact that the hood was propped up. She had always thought that was a sure sign of distress that would signal any passing motorist to stop and offer assistance. She was secretly glad, however, that the previous cars did not stop, not knowing what type of person she would encounter alone at 10:30 on a Thursday evening. She would just have to change this tire by herself, Lisa decided, and set herself to the task with new resolve.

Lisa had the spare on the ground by the side of the car and was preparing to jack up the right rear bumper, when a pair of headlights suddenly illuminated her work area. She could tell the truck was slowing down, and rose to meet the person getting out of the driver's seat. A tall man in a cowboy hat strode toward her, his boots jingling with each step. A huge knot suddenly formed in the pit of her stomach. In the lights of his vehicle, he could see her clearly, but she could only make out his silhouette, and she could not see if there was someone in the cab with him.

A tall figure continued toward her and she thought to pick up her flashlight and point it toward him. She squinted as the stranger tipped his hat, and called, "Evenin', ma'am." As he came closer, his eyes indicated he must have been smiling under his huge mustache. "You needin' some help?"

He was now towering over her, surveying the situation with calm. "Actually," she choked out, "Do you have a cell phone I could use to call my husband?" She put special emphasis on the last word.

The cowboy's eyes brightened, "You know, I just invested in one of those in town today! I'll be right back." He turned and hurried back to the cab, reappearing moments later with the phone in his hand, looking a little puzzled. "Eh... do you know how to use one of these?" He held out the phone uncertainly to her.

"Yes, thank you," she flashed a faint smile his way.

The stranger immediately set to work. "You just give your husband a jingle there and tell him the trouble you've had and that you'll be a little late, and I'll get this changed up for you right quick." He tipped his hat again as he stepped in front of her, after giving those cheerful instructions. He got right to work, seemingly unaware of her eye on him all during her phone conversation.

The strong man made short work of the tire change and was putting the tools away when she held out the phone to him.

"Thank you, very much." Lisa smiled weakly again and met his blue eyes.

He took the phone and slipped it into the front pocket of his western shirt, his gaze still locked on hers. He also seemed to notice her red nail polished fingernails. She was thankful that he had come by to help. She disliked breaking nails or chipping polish.

"Not a problem," he tipped his hat again.

What is this with the hat tipping? Lisa thought.

"Well, there you go... you're all set. But I wouldn't run it too fast on that doughnut. You're not going far, are you?" he closed the hatch of the van after setting the old tire and tools in the back floor.

"No," she hesitated, "No, just into Alpine."

"That should be OK, then. I'm goin' on past there, so I'll just stay behind you on the road and make sure you don't have anymore trouble." his voice was deep and reassuring.

Lisa didn't refuse his offer. She was used to following a man's leadership. "Uh ... how much do I owe you?" she questioned as the tall muscular man in the Stetson hat turned to leave. He turned to face her directly. "Owe me?" he sounded confused.

"For changing the tire."

She watched a twinkle start in his eye and spread until the corners of his great mustache rose a little, and presumed he must be smiling again. "Let's just say this one is on the house," he drawled, "I'm always happy to help out a lady in distress, ma'am." Again he touched the brim of his hat before turning and getting behind the wheel of his truck.

***

He had left off the word pretty before lady, not because she wasn't. No, her beauty had been the first thing he had noticed as he had walked up to her shortly before. But he had seen the ring on her finger, and heard the ...h... word mentioned, and just the sting of hearing it had left him unable to think further about her beauty, her long brown hair, her painted nails and those big teary eyes. *No!* He caught his mind traveling, and willed it to stay on the taillights of the car in front of him.

The cowboy hoped the sight of his headlights in her rear view mirror would comfort her during the ten miles into Alpine. When she reached the second intersection on the other side of town and made a left, he flashed his bright lights and honked one short honk on his horn, as he sped off into the clearing night.

2

Coming home from a bull sale, AC and his foreman Hobbie stopped at the Bear Wallow Café in Alpine. They had traveled through the night, and a quick breakfast and coffee to go would hold them the rest of the way to the ranch, where Hobbie's wife, Emma, would be sure to have Sunday dinner waiting. AC thought about stopping at the little church for services, but decided for Hobbie's sake that they were both too tired and ragged looking. They strolled leisurely to the truck now, when AC noticed a familiar vehicle parked across the street in front of the Country Store. Presently, a woman glided out of the store with a Sunday paper in her hand. Her wavy brown hair billowed over her shoulders to fall over a floral print dress. The sight sent a warm shiver down AC's spine. She entered the van, pulled out, and turned the corner right in front of him and Hobbie. Her van was packed with children, it seemed, and the image of a little blonde boy with his face pressed against the side rear window immediately impressed itself on his mind. There was no doubt that this was the woman he had helped last week, but he was quick to push aside any emotion that he felt rising within himself.

"You OK, AC?" Hobbie asked, while moving the toothpick deftly about in his mouth. "You look a mite pale."

"Uh...yea...fine," AC cleared his throat. He nudged Hobbie in the ribs. "I reckon we ought to get this ol' boy on down to his new home." He quickened his pace to the truck.

3

Lisa Taff twirled her brown curls absently around her left, red nail-polished index finger. Some would call her hair a dark shade of blonde, but she called it a "mousy" brown. Amid growing frustration, she closed the notebook before her a little too forcefully, and pushed her books away.

During the first five years that she had been married to Grant Taff, she had gotten an advanced degree in Psychology and joined a private counseling practice, in addition to having their first two children. When their third child was on the way, Grant had convinced her to stay at home as a full time mom. He had become, after all, a successful artist and sculptor, and was becoming quite popular in the Southwestern states, as well as back east. To her surprise, she actually enjoyed mothering their children full time and keeping their home. But now, with five children, and a widow at age 34, she felt she had to go back to school to try to get a school counselor's license in order to get a job and support the family.

Four years earlier, when she and Grant had moved their family out of the city and to Alpine, she had envisioned living their lives for a while in relative calm, giving Grant some inspiration and raising their four boys and baby girl, (and who knows how many more little ones) in the small town atmosphere of the quaint little mountain village, at least until they were ready to return to city opportunities. They had purchased a roomy cabin, with a large windowed room that Grant used for a studio. He had contracted with several local and area galleries and gift shops for his paintings and graphics, and had also started to teach a few Art classes at the community college in Springerville. They managed to have a good income from Grant's artwork, teaching, and some wise investing in their early marriage.

The town people, and especially the church family, had been extremely helpful and kind when, two years earlier, Grant had collapsed unexpectedly from a heart attack, and died the following morning. Lisa was devastated, unable even to comfort her own children for several days. She was sure that only her faith in God had carried her through those first days, weeks and months. God and a few close friends had continued to be her strength and help. Brent Beem, one of the owners of the local gallery where Grant had much of his work, had helped her with financial matters, and continued the marketing of Grant's work. He had been at her right hand to help in any way. Although Brent was very handsome and popular in town and attended the church, she assured herself she was not ready to forsake her memory of Grant and his place in her heart so soon. She still ached for Grant- his tender arms, his quiet laugh, and his endless energy and creative flair. Oh, how she missed him. How she feared not missing him.

4

Riding his best horse, Blaze, AC checked the heifers and fence line on the eastern border of his sprawling ranch on the Blue River. He had trouble concentrating on even this simple task. The image of the little blonde boy peering out the back window of that van in Alpine refused to be pushed aside. A certain sadness covered his heart, as his memory took him back to his own childhood. He remembered himself at five years old, gazing out the back seat window of the family station wagon, as they followed the hearse down the long road to the cemetery. He had looked out the window and watched the scenery without really seeing it, the ache in his heart so severe, the tears clouding any vision.

His dad had been his hero, able to ride like the wind and punch cattle like no one else. He was a champion roper and skilled horse breaker. AC, at five, had been six feet tall when in his father's presence, the older man's voice always ringing with praise and affirmation for his eight children; his eyes always sparkling, like he was about to spill a well kept secret.

When that demon of a horse his dad had been working on bucked him off and trampled him to death, AC's world had crumbled. Only when his dad's younger brother, Clay, married his mother and took on the responsibility of his brother's children, did the world right itself a bit in the child's eyes. Clay looked like AC's daddy, and had his same voice and smile. Although he took on all the children and treated them with fairness, Clay seemed to have had a tender spot in his heart for his little namesake.

Clay had raised AC and his brothers and sisters up fine. He raised them with a strong work ethic, a strong play ethic and a strong faith in God and his everyday working in their lives. AC had loved Clay every bit as much as he had his dad. He had helped him through many heartbreaks.

When his high school sweetheart went off to college on a rodeo scholarship and came back with a high-falooting rodeo cowboy in tow, Clay helped him through his broken heart. When AC suddenly found out that the lady he was about to give an engagement ring to, already had a husband, it was Clay, again, who helped him put the pieces of himself together. But when Clay died, AC thought his only option was to get away. His brothers and sisters would take care of his mother and the ranch. He needed to escape.

Now, thoughts of the young woman on the road- the young *married* woman on the road and the little boy in the back of her van haunted him. He ached for home; he ached for Clay and mama. His own fragile heart ached within him with every beat. He couldn't, wouldn't let these intruding thoughts stay in his mind.

5

Hobbie and Emma were in the kitchen when AC came out of his bedroom and followed his nose to the sweet aroma of bacon, eggs, and buttermilk biscuits. He helped himself to some fresh coffee, while Emma eyed him with a raised eyebrow.

AC had on a new pair of crisp jeans, a black western shirt and a maroon bandana around his neck. His blonde waves were damp and finger combed.

Hobbie was the first to break the silence. "You look almost handsome, all spiffed up like you are." He peeked over his coffee cup as he sat at the wooden table. When AC made no comment, he continued, "Would that be because the meetin' is at Miss Hinkle's today? Has she finally gotten to you with them yellow curls?" his grin covered his face, no longer hidden by the coffee cup.

"Melissa Hinkle makes me nervous." AC said flatly. "I was of a mind to go in to Alpine today."

"Alpine!" Emma nearly shouted. "Why, we haven't been there since we started the meetings down here. That'll be four years come spring."

"I reckon so," AC mused. "I just want to see if Preacher Woods is still there."

"Oh, he is," Emma replied, "Though the missus' health isn't too good right now. I hear their boys are takin' turns coming from Show Low to look out after them both...recoverin' from surgery I think."

"I'd best pay them a call, then." AC stated. He pressed his mustache down with his thumb and first finger and grabbed his Stetson off its peg. "I expect I'll be back around three," he said, jamming his hat on his head.

"Shall I give Miss Hinkle your regards? I know she'll comment on missin' ya." Hobbie winked as AC passed him, and headed out.

"Sure," he murmured as he walked out the door.

AC loaded himself in his Silverado quad cab pick-up and started up the road to the sleepy town of Alpine. As he eased up the road, he let his thoughts wander, albeit not too far. Suddenly he questioned his motives. Why exactly was he going to Alpine? Brother Woods probably would not even remember him. He had only been to the Alpine church twice. Hobbie and Emma were the ones that knew him and many of the folks in Alpine, having lived on this side of the Blue for some time. Was it that he suspected that the "lady in distress" from a couple of weeks ago went there? She had said that she was married, so he had no intentions of following her around. Yet, something within was calling, urging him to go on. Maybe she knew of someone who needed his help. Maybe
she would lead him to whatever was pulling at his heart and spirit. Clay and his mother had taught him to listen to God and inner leading. While he hadn't done much of it himself, he had certainly tagged along on enough of Clay's trips to visit people or go certain places, all on the leading of these inner promptings that Clay recognized as the Lord speaking to him. Clay's leading had always taken him to the right places at the right times to either give or receive just what was needed.

No, he decided, that beautiful woman probably was not the key, since she had shared what she had, but perhaps she held the key to him getting involved with someone else. Maybe she had a sister just as pretty and sweet as she seemed? Now AC was really letting his mind wander.

AC realized that he hadn't timed it right when he heard singing and slipped inside the small church to find a place on the back pew. He figured he would listen to the singing rather than join in just yet. Upon sitting down, he immediately spotted his "woman in distress" seated at the end of a pew full of children. Next to her sat a black haired man. Quite a family, he thought to himself. He quickly counted four boys in the pew. After a few more songs, Brother Woods instructed everyone to greet each other. AC was lost in a mass of handshakes and greetings. Suddenly he felt a persistent pounding in the area of his thigh. AC looked down to see the face of the little blonde- haired boy that had been haunting his mind the last week.

"Well, howdy..." AC smiled down at the boy and then crouched down to meet his gaze straight on.

"Howdy." the boy was solemn. "Are you a real cowboy?"

"Well now, I figure I am... yes indeed." AC flashed a big grin at the small boy again. His hair was slicked down with a neat side part and he had on a sport shirt and dress pants with loafers on his feet.

"My brother is a real cowboy too!" he beamed. "He has one of those scarves, too, and a genuine cowboy hat, too!" The excitement radiated from the little boy, who spoke of his brother with pride.

Before AC could respond, the boy spouted out, "Gotta go!" and bolted back to the pew where his family was already seated. The service progressed in its usual format, and when the special music was scheduled, AC was surprised to see his "lady in distress" take a small girl from her lap, set her in the pew, and proceed to the front to sing.

***

It took several moments for Lisa to notice and then recognize the tall visitor in the back pew. However did he manage his way back into her world? He sat in the area where she usually tried to focus whenever she sang. She had found that if she focused on a spot at the back of the sanctuary, she had less of a problem with her nerves. Not so today. His wavy blonde hair hung atop an inch or so of pale light skin, which promptly gave way to a line of brown tan about midway down his forehead. A sudden jolt rocked her and her heart raced. She was nervous singing this song, and tried to collect herself, as the musical intro to the song rang out. Still, she wondered who the man hiding behind the huge sandy mustache at the back of the church was.

***

Once again, this beautiful woman stirred something deep within AC. He didn't even hear the words she sang, but rather, latched on to the fall of her hair partially up in combs on each side. The subtle make-up, painted nails and lips begged his thoughts down a course he knew was wrong. *Her husband is sitting just a few rows in front of me, and here I am thinking this way! And in church yet!*

Her clear voice started the chorus and the words fairly knocked him out. She sang:

17

"He will never leave us
Like orphans in the storm…"

His heart pitched and his head suddenly was clear. He paid attention easily to the rest of the song and allowed it to minister to his innermost hurt. Lisa herself choked on those very words, and although the tears suddenly flowed, she regained composure quickly. AC could not look at the singer anymore. He bowed his head in front of himself and felt two drops on his new jeans.

After service, AC intended to slip out quietly, but a matronly saint who insisted he stay for potluck cornered him. He tried to convince her that he had not brought a dish, and really should be getting along, but she simply said, "There's enough in the pot that I brought for you, young man." as she herded him back into the church.

The little blonde-haired boy rescued him from the older woman's clutches by grabbing his other hand, the one holding his hat, and dragging him toward his lovely mother.

"Hey, Matthew! This man is a real cowboy!" he said triumphantly.

AC figured the boy suddenly standing before him to be about 11 or 12 years old. He wore a man's white handkerchief tied around his neck and a multicolored western shirt. He wore badly scuffed old cowboy boots and carried a cowboy hat that looked like it had been tossed before a stampede. His expression was flat.

"That so?" his gaze pierced AC.

"I reckon so, yes, sir." He returned Matthews gaze and stuck out his hand. "Pleased to meet you."

A slow smile graced Matthew's face. "Yeah." He said as he shook AC's hand energetically. Matthew glanced to his left. "This is my mom," he said.

"Lisa." she smiled.

"Ma'am," AC said as he looked into her blue-green eyes. He held her hand perhaps a moment too long before he turned to the man beside her and said, "And this must be your Daddy." He pushed his hand out to the man.

"My daddy is up in heaven with Jesus," the younger boy said matter-of-factly.

"Oh." AC glanced from the man to Lisa and then to the boy.

The man cleared his throat, and Lisa jumped in, "This is Brent Beem, a friend of the family."

"A close family friend," Brent interjected, putting his arm around Lisa's shoulder and pulling her slightly closer. I run the gallery in town, across from Bear Wallow."

"Good to meet you," AC hoped that the flush he felt in his cheeks was not showing too much. He talked with them long enough to be introduced to the other children, Jacob, John, Peter, and Becky. He tried to mingle, then, to restore some order to his muddled brain and pounding heart.

After the meal, he again attempted to slip out quickly, but the small group of children playing in the front of the church somehow cornered him into playing with his lasso. It was in the back of his pick-up along with a saddle that needed fixing, that he had almost forgotten about. Before long, he was showing them roping moves, roping the corner of the church sign, and the handicapped parking sign. AC managed to slip away after the first few adults began to leave. The drive back to the ranch was long and filled with so many questions. He almost wished he had not gone to Alpine. Instead of relieving some of the inner turmoil, it had only made things worse.

6

Going to church over the next few weeks, AC noticed that he seemed to attract Matthew like a magnet. He could also see that Matthew was quite a handful, and indeed found plenty of trouble. He wasn't sure why the boy was attracted to him. Maybe it was because he was a real cowboy with a real ranch. Maybe it was because he dressed the part of a big Texas cowboy, although his blood ran Wyoming through and through. He could also see that the boy was 99.9% bravado. What troubled him most, however, was that in all this vision that he seemed to have into the boy, his heart caught glimpses of himself at a much younger age.

It was in those glimpses, replayed over and over in his mind on many sleepless nights that he realized why the Lord must have urged him to go to the Alpine church. He was to help this boy. It was out of this revelation that he approached Lisa with the idea of Matthew helping out at his ranch.

"I'm thinking of hiring on the Taff boy on the weekends." AC had said, running a hand through his stray waves.

Hobbie sighed, "I don't know what's got into you, boss."

AC chuckled, "Why, what do you mean, Hobbie?"

"What with you runnin' in to Alpine all the time, and now talkin' of hirin' this boy and all. It's not like you to go chasin' all over like that. Why, I'm goin' to have to get the fuel man in here again pretty soon the way you are suckin' up all the petrol!" Hobbie fussed.

"I reckon I'll take care of paying the bills. Hobb, you just order what we need," AC said calmly.

"And how are you goin' to hire this boy on?" Hobbie queried.

"I figure maybe I could trade him work for one of Missy's colts. She's due here pretty quick."

"Missy's colt! We can't spare no horses!" Hobbie argued.

"I reckon Russ or Dustie will give me a good deal on some 2 year olds of theirs."

"You know your kin ain't goin' to bring no horses down here from clear up in Wyomin'. None of 'em ever even been out here to visit since you got the place. 'Cept for your momma, bless her heart."

"Then it is about high time they pay me a visit, isn't it?" He pressed his mustache down and jammed the hat on his head as he walked out.

***

Rita flipped the sign in the window to "OPEN" and pulled the library door toward her, as Lisa and three of her children bounced up the sidewalk of the Alpine Public Library to greet her

"You are just in time," she half-laughed, half-spoke.

"Yea. Mom said we had to wait until after lunch, so we ate fast," the little sandy-haired boy sang out.

"Well, come right on in. I saved your favorite Tigger chair for you. Go into the story room and make yourselves at home," Rita instructed the three youngsters.

If it was one thing Lisa insisted upon in her household, it was reading time and frequent trips to the library. She felt very satisfied that all her children, even Becky, at 4, had a passion for reading. The children ran into the room, as Lisa and Rita found chairs and huddled together behind the large checkout desk like schoolgirls.

"I've been waiting for you to come in, where have you been?" Rita bubbled.

"And I've been longing to speak to someone over 10," Lisa laughed. "The library schedule and my schedule just haven't meshed in the last week or so. How have you been?"

"Oh, great, great… and you?"

"Like I said, I've been starved for adult conversation."

"Well, here I am, girl, start talking."

The two visited and giggled, thankful that it was a slow Thursday afternoon at the library.

"So, I have a question about this Mr. Greening guy, Rita, do you know anything about him?"

"Well, he bought that ranch about 5 years ago, but the couple that works for… or with him have been here forever. They are wonderful. The guy who owned the ranch before lived back east… came out in the spring every year to brand, and then went back east. Hobbie and Emma pretty much ran the whole operation for him. They are so cute." Rita's easy laugh rang through the quiet library. "Anyway, the guy back east... I can't recall his name, he ran into some money problems and had to lay off Hobbie and Emma and sell the ranch. That's when Mr. Greening bought it. I don't know much about him, but he did keep Hobbie and Emma on... that is one good thing I can say about him. They don't know anything but ranching."

"Hmm. So do you think I should let Matthew and Jacob go down there for a day and help him out? He offered to take the boys and show them around his ranch, since Matthew is going through this phase. By the way, it is your fault, you know, that I am even in this predicament... you giving Matthew all those Stephen Bly westerns. "

"Stephen Bly happens to be my favorite author," Rita laughed.

"Mr. Greening seems nice enough. You don't think he is creepy or anything...do you?"

"Emma and Hobbie are good people, Lisa," Rita smiled, "I think it is pretty nice of him to offer Mathew to see a real working ranch, since he is so interested in the whole cowboy and western lifestyle. Who knows, it might be just what he needs. And the only thing creepy about him is that he doesn't visit the library very often," Rita burst out laughing, and Lisa had no choice but to join in.

"So how are you really, Lisa?" Rita suddenly became uncharacteristically serious.

"Well that was a sudden jump. Why so serious?"

"I don't know, Lisa, I am just a little worried about you. Are you OK?"

24

"Sometimes I think I am doing great, really sailing along, and others…well I feel like I am about to fall to pieces. Brent helps out a lot. If I need anything fixed or have any problem or anything, I can call on him. He is very helpful, and he is still carrying and marketing Grant's works through the gallery." Lisa hesitated. "I think he is interested in our relationship going deeper."

"And you?"

"I do like him, I have to admit, but I am still conflicted. He can get pretty pushy."

"Well don't you let him, girl. If you need space, you let him know. Don't let that man push you around. Don't you let any man push you around, you hear?"

***

Lisa had been leery of the proposition at first, but with some gentle persuasion on AC's part, and fervent encouragement on Brent's part, she allowed Matthew to work out a schedule of times that he would work with AC on his ranch. Lisa seemed at little uncomfortable with the entire arrangement. However, the instant relief that both she and Matthew seemed to get from the initial few days of Matthew being on the ranch must have over ridden her better judgment about her son getting involved with some cowboy type.

It appeared to AC that each week brought Lisa and Brent closer together, as he observed them at church and briefly at times during the transfer of Matthew. That did not bother AC, because he was already beginning to see glimmers of light in the child's eyes. Lisa was attractive, all right, and during his waking hours he found himself pushing thoughts of her out of his head, but push them he did. Brent and Lisa appeared serious about a relationship, and he would not allow himself to interfere. Besides, AC felt confident that the boy was his mission. They rode together in the pasture now, the afternoon sun behind them.

"You like it here?" AC looked over at the boy, sitting tall in his saddle.

"Yes, I do"

"How long you been in Alpine?'

"About 4 years, I guess. We moved up here from Phoenix just after my sister was born. My dad was real popular in Phoenix, but we came up here so he could paint more… get more inspiration"

This was the most the boy had spoken in all the times he had been to the ranch. Mostly he simply nodded or gave short answers, or simply listened. It seemed as if the boy was soaking up all the information, all the daily ranch life that he could. He was definitely interested in playing the part of a cowboy, but AC was interested in showing him the life of a cowboy, and hoped he would enjoy the real part of it. He remembered riding with Clay.

"Tell me about you. What else do you like?"

"I like to read, and play, I don't know."

"Readin' and playin' is good, what else?"

"I like looking at my dad's paintings."

"You like painting, too?"

"No, just looking."

"You got a favorite one?'

"Yea."

"What is it of…you?'

"No. He painted scenery and wildlife, not people."

"So what is your favorite one?"

"The last one he did. It is of a mother and baby elk. I have the picture on my bedpost, I keep it there to remember him, but the painting from it is in my mom's closet. She keeps it there, way in the back. I look at it sometimes."

"How come she is keeping it in the closet?"

"It isn't signed. He didn't get to sign it."

"Hmm."

"I don't know if she is keeping it in there to remember my dad… or to forget him."

7

"You want me to farm out my children??" Lisa's voice was louder than she anticipated, and Brent immediately grabbed her arm, leading her to the front of the house and away from the bedrooms that she had just gotten the children settled in.

"Shh," he said harshly. "There is no cause to raise your voice. You just admitted that Matthew was causing problems in school again. This is just the type of discipline and organization that he needs. They won't allow him any slack at Westridge."

"He's having problems, not causing problems." Lisa murmured weakly.

Brent held her close, and Lisa rested her head against his shoulder. "Matthew, Jacob and Peter all need strong authority in their lives. You can't give that, and you know they don't respond to me. I can't take on all these kids, Lisa," he stated logically.

"But I already lost Grant, and I can't just give away my boys too!" she moaned into Brent's shoulder.

"Grant has been gone for 2 years." Brent commented, annoyance obvious in his tone, "And you are not giving the older boys away. They will just be in Colorado. They come home on holiday breaks. You can call them weekly. You are just thinking of them. This is what they need. The structure and camaraderie will be good for them." Brent held Lisa close, rubbing her back gently with both hands. His hand moved up through her long chestnut hair. His lips found her cheek as he caressed her, trying to calm her anger at the proposition he had made. She slumped to his embrace and he knew he was getting to her. She had been too long without Grant, and he could tell.

"It will be good for us," he whispered into her ear, as his hands searched for something he wanted. Lisa almost succumbed. Then a reaction boiled within her, and she finally jerked away from Brent's arms.

"So that is what this is about?" She stared angrily at Brent's surprised face. "You want me to get rid of my kids so things will be better for us?" Anger flashed once again.

Brent stepped forward to correct his mistake. "You know I love you, Lisa." He gathered her, "You said you would consider marrying me," He spoke against her ear, and the warmth of his breath must have startled her. His dealings with her were crippling her resolve, as he worked quickly to ply her body and emotions to his will. "We don't want the family torn apart, do we?" His hands went where she obviously did not want them to go, but her voice halted in her throat. "It would be best for us all... everyone," he nudged closer, "You know I can't take on all these kids," he whispered as he felt he was finally getting her to the place he wanted her. But he had misspoken again. She seemed to gather her shattered wits and slid out of his grasp, quickly walking out of reach.

"Stay there," she commanded. "If you take on me, Brent, the kids are a package deal, you get all of them. You don't have to adopt them, but we need to be together as a family."

"If Matthew stays here, he will tear the family apart." Brent said bluntly, chagrined that she had stepped out of his embrace.

"And if he goes, it will tear the family apart, too." Lisa was firm, but Brent could tell that she was not beyond convincing on this. He smiled as he mentally pulled himself back together.

"Why don't you just think about it," his tone gentled as he stepped closer, "We don't have to decide right this minute." He had quickly lessened the distance between them and again was close enough to Lisa for her to feel his breath on her cheek. "Sleep on it," he pressed his lips on her cheek, then stepped quickly to the door and out into the night.

***

Sleep eluded Matthew long after he heard his mother close the door to her room. He crept out into the living room with his flashlight and examined the brochure and paperwork lying on the table in the corner of the room. He would just have to try to do better in school. His life depended on it.

***

Lisa woke from restless sleep at the first light of dawn. She rose to push the curtain of her bedroom window aside. She loved the dawn. Sun set was a close second, but daylight had always been more comforting to her than darkness. As she watched the morning bloom, she saw a small herd of elk enter the pasture beyond their cabin. Elk always filled her heart with awe. She remembered the last painting that Grant had done. The one that hid, finished except for the artist's signature in the right corner, at the back of her closet. It was a cow elk at the edge of the herd, nuzzling her newborn calf. Matthew had the picture it was taken from taped to his bedpost. Matthew had been with Grant on that picture taking expedition, as he usually was. Matthew loved nature and all the animals that were found in it.

He had grown up tagging along with Grant on his many outings of taking pictures that he would use as a basis from which to build his paintings. Outdoors was where Matthew felt most at home. That had been one of the reasons they had chosen Alpine to settle. There was an abundance of scenery and wildlife to spark Grant's creativity, and also an abundance of nature to romp in to satisfy Matthew's active curiosity.

Images of Grant and Matthew only made the demands of Brent that much more difficult. How could she possibly decide what to do?

8

"Let them go," AC said as he closed Lisa's car door for her. She had a worried look on her face as she watched all of her children suddenly disappear. "He just wants to show them some braiding that he has been working on today."

She watched her children run after Matthew, not able to keep back a smile, obviously pleased with their excitement.

"You are planning on coming to the branding the end of the month, aren't you?" AC interrupted Lisa's motherly thoughts.

"Yes, I guess so," she turned toward him, and AC was almost dumbstruck by her smile.

"The boy says you're planning on sending him to a military school or something up in Colorado," he blurted out. The news had troubled him so much, he had to get it out.

"*The boy* has a name, Mr. Greening," Lisa returned hotly, "Why don't you use it?"

AC's heart wrenched and he feared his expression betrayed his pain. When talking directly to Matthew, he always called him "young man", never daring to use his name. He could not be that personal with him. He could not admit to himself or anyone else, for that matter, that he cared deeply for the boy- loved him even, and longed to hug away his hurt, as Clay had done for him so many years ago. No, to call him by his name would be to get too personal. It would be to risk admitting that he longed to love this boy like a son. And he could not allow himself to do that.

"I think the boy is mighty put out by it, ma'am." AC struggled to keep his composure.

"The boy's name is Matthew!" Lisa pressed.

"Do you need a man that bad?" he shot at her, "to send him away when he needs you?" Instantly he regretted his words, but it was too late to take them back. They hung in the air like icicles, and made him swallow hard. He shouldn't have said them. He should not have betrayed the boy's trust. He had known, after all, the pain of losing someone, the feeling of being adrift on the ocean on a small piece of wood. He knew the longing to fill the void and replace the part of you that was forever gone. He should have shown her more compassion. At least more tact, but his heart ached for the boy and for himself.

His words could have been the palm of his hand slapping her face for the damage they had done. Her fury built in the pit of her soul. She knew the words were true even before he had said them. "My personal life is NONE of your business!" her eyes flashed fire, and she wished she could think of something harsh and hurtful to say back, but no words came. Only tears, and she was determined not to let them fall. She leaned into the van and blew the horn long and loud.

Suddenly AC wanted to reach for her, to embrace her and whisper sincere apology and into her ear. He wanted to stroke her silky hair. He longed to love her, but he dared not. As the children filtered back to the van, he said lowly, "Go ahead and bring that boyfriend of yours along to the branding.

He may be a sorry fella, but I sure could use all the pairs of hands I can get." He turned and walked to the house, murmuring something to Matthew as he passed him.

AC sat at the table with his head in his hands. Emma touched him gently on the shoulder. "He's a good boy, that Matthew."

"I know," AC looked pleadingly into Emma's kind face. "He's hurting. He is scared to death she will send him off somewhere. He is trying to be good. Why can't his mama see that?"

"Maybe she is hurting too bad herself."

9

The sun was high overhead, and the dust was rolling as AC herded the next batch of calves into the corral near the branding fire. Hobbie was in charge of the branding irons, holding one in each hand. A neighbor held the inoculation syringes ready, and his wife, Kathy, stood at the head of the calf table with the de-horner. Emma alternately passed Kathy the ear tags. AC's ranch hand, Jimmy-Joe was one of the legmen, cutting the bulls swiftly, while holding their leg. Matthew was the other legman, helping Jimmy-Joe hold the calves steady. Lisa could tell that Matthew was in his element, as she and the rest of the children watched the operations from a rail fence. He was having the time of his life. He had developed a skill in working with the animals, quickly obeying any instructions that were barked at him by the no-nonsense cowboys on AC's ranch, and gobbling frequent praise that came in the form of nods of approval, pats on the back, or subtle glances, movements or twitches of sort. Even the occasional words that were spoken were not discernable as praise to Lisa, but she could tell by watching the sparkle in Matthew's eyes that he had just been affirmed.

Emma had enlisted the help of Jacob in laying out the ear tags in the right order and loading the tag gun, but Lisa and the younger children sat on the outskirts of the branding area. Lisa was atop the corral fence and the children behind it, peering through the rails. They were fascinated by all the workings of this busy time, and were content to watch wide-eyed from the sidelines. The sights and smells at times made Lisa reel with queasiness, but she often closed her eyes, figuring no one was paying attention to her anyway.

She was right. Everyone was too busy to pay too much attention to anything but his or her specific task. Everyone but AC. He stole glances every now and then at Lisa to make sure she was OK. He knew from watching her that the whole ordeal was probably overwhelming to her, and half expected her to faint at any time. She sported her usual glossy, almost red nail polish, and bright white tennis shoes. They would not stay that way for long. He had privately told Arlene, the wife of one of his hands, to keep an eye out for her.

AC was a little surprised that Lisa had not brought Brent along, but he was relieved. He did not need a greenhorn trying to prove anything to Lisa in front of him. Lisa had seemed a little less antagonistic toward him this morning, however. He was not sure whether that was due to a true change in the way she thought of him or merely the outrageously early hour he had requested them to be there. For all he knew, she could have still been asleep.

He had been keeping an eye on her throughout the morning, stealing glances, watching her as she worked with her children. He wanted several times to sidle up next to her as she sat atop the fence and slip his arm around her waist, to smell the scent of her silky hair that he had gotten a brief whiff of this morning, when it was still damp. He wanted her. For a friend at least, for a lover at best. There was just the small problem of Brent, not to mention the larger one, of the fact that Lisa did not like AC. He had pushed all those thoughts to the corner of his heart as he worked the calves. He was not one to push his point, to push himself on anyone else uninvited, yet he found himself pressing for things like he never would have before. He knew his mission was with the boy, but he began to think more and more of the boy's mother.

What had made him even suggest that Matthew come to the ranch and work? What had caused him to invite him and his family to come for the day of branding? What had driven him to incur Lisa's wrath to take up for the boy to the extent that he had rudely insulted her? He was losing control of something on the inside, being taken over by some force deep within him that he was not sure he wanted to come out. He trembled at the thought of being able to handle what seemed to be happening, but it appeared too late to be able to do anything about it.

AC saw the young bull out the corner of his eye. He was larger than any of the rest had been. *Maybe just a bit too big for that calf table...Maybe I ought to tell Hobbie to do him on the ground at the last...Aw, I guess he'll be all right.* AC hurried to close the chute behind the calves he and Ray had just corralled. Then it was too late. They had clamped the bull down as best they could, and the helping neighbor's strength pulled the table horizontal, although the calf was not quite secure. AC watched in silent fear, as the next moments seemed to pass in slow motion. Hobbie pressed the hot irons into the animal's hide as Kathy pierced his ear. That was as far as the operation got. In a split second, the calf had wrenched his legs free from Jimmy-Joe and Matthew's control. Jimmy-Joe's knife went flying and the bull delivered two quick kicks to Matthew's head before he could get clear, one to the forehead, and one to the temple.

AC was at Matthew's fallen body first, without knowing how he had gotten there. The bull was instantly back on the ground bawling, and herded away. Lisa was over her son's limp shape an instant later, and cries of panic and concern filled the air. AC jerked into autopilot and started shouting commands.

Within 10 minutes, they had stopped the profuse flow of blood, iced both wounds and carefully attached Matthew's head and upper body to a piece of plywood. Dr. Wright, an MD who owned the small ranch next to AC's was not up for the weekend, but Hobbie had called for an ambulance intercept in Alpine when Matthew did not come to. He was slowly loaded into the Silverado, his head in Lisa's lap and his feet stretched out onto AC's lap in front of the wheel. Emma poked her head in the window on Lisa's side, looking into her panic stricken face.

"Don't you worry none about these precious little ones here. We'll take care of them just fine," she said firmly, "You just get that one there fixed up right." She nodded at Matthew and patted a plump hand on Lisa's shoulder, "The Lord is good, Mrs. Taff, He'll take care of it all." Lisa nodded through watery eyes as AC threw the truck into gear and raced up the dirt road to Alpine.

AC prayed and Lisa sat silently. Suddenly she struck out fiercely. " I knew something like this would happen! I knew I should never have let him do all this cowboy stuff! This was such a *stupid* idea to let him get involved in all of this!" she accused, lifting a hand to her temple.

He let her rage as he sped up. The road took several sharp turns, but AC kept up his speed. He had to get Matthew to help!

"You're making me sick!" Lisa snapped, casting another glare in his direction. AC immediately took his foot off the accelerator. The road would smooth out up ahead a ways, and it would do no good to have Lisa sick all over the place. She was probably woozy after the morning's activities anyway. AC looked at Lisa with concern and compassion. After a while he asked quietly, "Is that better?"

His mustache prevented her from fully seeing his expression, as usual, but his eyes were full of tenderness, and she seemed to relax a little. She bit her bottom lip and said softly, "I've already lost one man I loved ...I can't bear to lose another." Her teary eyes overflowed again. AC handed her a clean handkerchief from his pocket, and let his hand rest on hers, which was covering both of Matthew's, atop his barely moving chest.

"We are not going to lose Matthew," he said simply. Had he said we? Matthew wasn't even his to lose, and here he was carrying on like this. AC feared that Lisa had noticed the "we" too.

***

They arrived at the pavement on the outskirts of Alpine to find an ambulance ready and waiting. The transfer of the young patient was swift. "I can only take one in the back," the EMT looked quickly at Lisa and AC. Lisa climbed in without a word, as AC helped her. He gripped her hand as she sat. "I'll be right behind you," his eyes found a place deep within her. She could barely see his faint smile of assurance under his large mustache. She thought for a moment to tell him that he didn't have to come along, but she merely nodded her head. Suddenly she knew that she did want him to follow. She wanted him in the back of the ambulance with Matthew and her.

Now what was she thinking, she chided herself many miles down the road. Did she need a man in her life so badly that she would allow this rancher a place in her heart? He himself had asked her the question. Did she need a man in her life? No. What she needed was to concentrate on Matthew and her children and their future together. Grant was gone, and she had to finally accept that and move on with her life with the precious gifts that he had left behind. She would concentrate on them and their life together, she determined, and nothing else. She and Brent had somewhat agreed to a slowing of their relationship, and now she would busy herself and her life once again with her children. If only Matthew would pull through this all right.

10

AC had not figured on driving the truck so much that day, and as a result had to stop in Springerville for gas. He always kept his truck topped off. Why had it been near empty when he needed it the most? He chastised himself about the gas, the branding accident, his feelings for Lisa, and everything else he could think of all the way to the Show Low Hospital.

He arrived at the hospital well after the ambulance, and was not allowed into the emergency room. He waited in the waiting room for what seemed ages. No one could give him answers about Matthew's condition. He called Emma at the ranch to check on the other children and tell them everyone had arrived in Show Low safely. He talked at length with Hobbie, who assured him that the boys at the branding could handle the rest of it that afternoon and the following day, if necessary. Emma would keep the younger ones in the house.

It was already dark when a nurse called his name in the waiting room, and beckoned him to follow her. She led him the semi-private room, and ushered him to a place beside Matthew's bed, opposite his mother.

"He keeps slipping in and out, but he keeps asking for you." Her voice was cautious and her gaze cool.

AC took the little hand in his. It was already starting to get calloused from the ranch work he had been doing. AC decided right then to get the boy some better working gloves. He spoke softly, next to the boy's ear, "How ya doin' fella? It's me, AC."

The boy's eyes shot open. His lips turned into a weak smile. "I'm real sorry about that calf, Mr. Greening," he managed.

"Hey, now," AC interrupted, "I told ya before that all the hands call me AC."

The boy nodded and half smiled.

"And don't go apologizing over that little bull, Matty. I shoulda cut him out and done him on the ground. He was too big for that calf table, Matty. I'm real sorry I didn't pay more attention before all the ruckus. Hey, the fact that you can remember all that is a good sign, huh?" His way was gentle.

"Matty?" the boy questioned lowly.

"Matty?" Lisa shot a baffled look at AC.

He had used the term of endearment without thinking. It had just flowed out of his mouth as if it belonged there and was supposed to slide out. He cleared his throat and drew away from the boy a little. "Well, we call Hobbs- Hobbie, and Jimmy -Joe's given name is really James Joseph, so ...it just seemed kinda OK to call ya Matty..." he recovered gruffly, "Hope that is OK with you, young man." Matthew just smiled and nodded. He seemed to be slipping again. AC looked to Lisa, panic in his eyes.

"The doctor said that he might drift in and out of consciousness. Hopefully the ins will be longer than the outs," she commented.

AC returned to the boy as he opened his eyes again. "You just go ahead and rest, young man, so you can get up and around again soon. We still got lots to do on the ranch..."

"He is NOT going to..." Lisa interjected vehemently, but she was silenced by a fiery glare from AC.

"And Missy is about to drop that colt of yours," he continued.

"Oh, yeah," Matty's eyes brightened and he struggled to sit up, but AC gentled him back down.

"You just be still and work on getting that knot on your head better, you hear?"

Matty nodded. Then his eyes flew open again. "AC, I've been wondering something a long time, and I better ask before I die...OK?" His voice was quiet and shaky.

"You are not going to die, Matty," AC stated firmly, "The Lord is taking care of you, remember?" Matty nodded and grinned faintly.

"Now, what is your question?" AC asked.

"Well, since we're talking about names, what do the A and C in your name stand for?" Matty looked directly into AC's eyes, and AC thought he saw a hint of impishness there. He smoothed his mustache with his thumb and fingers, cleared his throat and leaned toward the boy again. "Now, this here is just between you 'n me, you understand, not for anybody else... eh...it stands for... Arlow Clayton...that's my given name, first and middle. The back of his neck and cheeks grew hot.

"Thanks," Matty said lowly, before drifting out again.

AC collected himself and raised his body straight. Lisa motioned for AC to follow her to the hall. Before she spoke, he said lowly, shifting his hat nervously in his hands, "I'd appreciate it, ma'am, if that little bit of information I told your son would, eh, just stay in that room there." He looked at his boot tips.

"Don't worry, Arlow, your secret is safe with me," there was a hint of irritation in her voice. She did not forget about the indignation that had caused her to feel the need to speak with him in private.

"What on earth do you think you are doing telling him about there being so much work to do on the ranch? Do you honestly think that there is **any** chance in the **world** that I will ever allow him to work there again?" she ranted.

"I was just giving him something to hang on to," AC defended. "Besides, you can't let an accident like this just get the best of you. You'll run around being scared to death of everything for the rest of your life. He won't do brandin' anymore for awhile, and I'll watch him closer..." he insisted. He knew she blamed him, and he should have been paying closer attention, but she couldn't take Matthew away now. He hoped that she wouldn't.

"I will not..."The nurse interrupted Lisa with some more paperwork.

Moments later, Lisa joined AC in the ICU waiting room. "They said I could spend the night in here," Lisa commented, "The doctor wants to keep him for several days. He wants to keep a check on a dark spot that showed up on the CAT scan. He says there may be some internal bleeding." There was worry in her voice and face, and it took everything AC had to keep from gathering her in his arms and soaking up her tears on his shirt and heart.

I'll get us some coffee, and we had best settle in for the night, then," AC glanced at his watch. "It's getting pretty late."

"Us?" Lisa demanded.

"Well, sure, I'll stay here with you tonight," he stated, amazed that she would think that he would leave. "The kids will be fine with Emma and Hobbie."

The kids! Lisa had forgotten about the other boys and Becky. Surely they would be nervous about spending the night in a strange place! They didn't have nightclothes...toothbrushes... anything! It was all too much to think about right now. What was she to do?

"I can't ask you to stay, Mr. Greening." She tried to sound polite.

"You aren't askin', ma'am... I'm offerin'," his eyes were intense, but Lisa couldn't read his expression fully because of that mustache. AC took a step toward Lisa. She met his gaze and felt her fortitude crumble.

"Oh, AC," she spoke softly, " I'm so scared."

He put his arm around her shoulder and drew her close. She rested her head on his strong chest. "The last time I was here... Grant didn't make it until the morning," she whispered, the memory flooding back upon her like a hurricane.

"Everything is going to be OK, ma'am, I know it is," he held her close, his action speaking comfort to her heart and soul.

Suddenly Lisa pulled away. She had almost forgotten that she was angry with AC for putting Matthew in danger. Of course she had allowed it, too, but that was beside the point. She had not realized how dangerous it was. She wiped her tear-streaked cheeks with her palms.

"Thank you, Mr. Greening, for bringing us here," she said stiffly, "And for...well...for watching the other children at the ranch tonight." Why did she have so much to thank him for, when she wanted to stay her distance?

"I'm glad to help, ma'am. I'll just let Emma know, and I'll be back to sit with you tonight."

"No," she snapped, not because she didn't want him there. No, she wanted him there...wanted him near her, holding her, but because she couldn't trust herself to hold the newly formed decisions she had just made. Besides, she was angry with him, and couldn't even trust herself to stay that way under his gentleness. "Please... go," she said firmly.

AC did not push her this time. He pulled an old feed slip out of his shirt pocket and scribbled something on it. "This is my cell phone number. Call if you need any help. I'll call in the morning to check on you," he grumbled, and shoved the paper toward her. She nodded and he stomped out of the room.

Lisa sank down into the overstuffed chair in a corner of the waiting room, her aloneness settling over her.

11

It was almost midnight when AC traipsed up the gravel driveway to the house. He encountered Emma sitting in soft lamplight in the rocking chair on the porch, a small bundle in her lap. She looked up at AC. "She's had a fitful night, the little darlin', all worried over every little thing."

"That's a mighty lot of worryin' for a little one to take on."

"The young'uns learn early sometimes."

AC held out his arms for the young girl, "You'd better get some sleep, Emma. Hobbie and this crew will be famished at first light." He looked kindly into the older woman's face as she transferred the blanketed girl into his embrace. He had left enough nieces in Wyoming to know how to cradle the small girl.

"Thank you, Emma. Thank you so much," he smiled wearily. "There is a jewel in your crown for today, Emma."

She chuckled as she made her way back into the house and to her room.

AC looked down into Becky's sleepy brown eyes. She smiled sheepishly.

"What's up, buttercup?" AC spoke quietly.

"I'm scared," Becky stated.

"Of what, darlin'?"

"Of Matthew, and Mommy, and spiders, and snakes, and big cows, and..."

"Whoa, little mite. That's a powerful lot to be worried about." AC interrupted.

Becky nodded and tucked her head back into AC's muscular chest.

"Well now," he began rocking again, "I know that your mama has told you that Jesus can do all our worryin' if we just let Him, and that sure does free us up to do a lot more of the fun stuff, right?"

She nodded against his chest.

"So, how about us lettin' Jesus do our worryin' for us tonight, OK? I just left Matthew and your mama, and they are both doin' fine. The doctor is goin' to keep Matthew there for a day or two, just to keep an eye on him. So how's about we ask Jesus to take over tonight, so you and I can get some sleep?"

"OK." Becky's voice was tiny.

AC began plainly, "Jesus, this here is AC and Becky, and we've got some mighty big things concernin' us tonight, and we'd be much obliged if you would just do our worryin' for us tonight, so as we could get some rest, and have us some fun in the mornin'. Thank you. Good night." AC brushed a kiss across the young girl's cheek.

"Ow," she sat facing him suddenly in his lap, and put a small hand on each shoulder. "I don't like your mustache. It scratches," she spoke firmly.

AC smoothed it with his thumb and fingers and tried to kiss her cheek again.

"Nope, still scratches," she announced.

"Well, no more kisses for you tonight then," he chuckled as he tucked her back against his shoulder. She snuggled, and within minutes was sound asleep.

AC sat for almost another hour rocking Becky before he gathered her and carried her to one of the upstairs bedrooms. He checked on the three boys, and then returned to his bedroom downstairs. He slid off his boots and lay wearily on top of the covers on his bed, after spending a considerable amount of time in the bathroom.

The smell of coffee a few hours later caused him to open one eye, but he refused to stir until the aroma of bacon and eggs hit his nostrils. Pulling himself off the bed took extreme effort, for he was exhausted both physically and mentally. He went to the bathroom to freshen up for the day, where he encountered the result of his rash actions of the past night. His reflection in the mirror made him cringe, and caused a surly attitude to flow over him, as he noticed a mound of wheat colored hair in the wastebasket.

He waited until he heard the children exit the kitchen to go and play before he entered the sweet smelling room. Hobbie was, surprisingly, still in the kitchen. AC waltzed over to the coffee pot, but before he could raise the cup to his lips, he heard the gasp from Emma, and Hobbie started in, "What in tarnation ever possessed you..?"

"Don't even go there!" AC snarled as he stomped out the door without filling his empty stomach.

12

AC sauntered down the hall of the hospital carrying several bags. If Lisa would not let Matty do real cowboying, he was at least going to look the part decently. If she could walk around in her high heels, matching nail polish and dangling earrings all the time, then Matty could look the part of a cowboy in style. He had been to the western store and bought a new maroon western shirt, some new Wranglers, a silk neckerchief, chinks, spurs, and leather boots. He had felt a twinge of guilt over the other children, so he had bought each one of them a neckerchief, and had even chosen a pretty red one for Lisa- to match her nail polish, of course.

He entered the semi-private room while Matty was being fed breakfast by his mother. Matty immediately stopped eating and pushed his mom away, obviously embarrassed at AC catching him being fed.

"Hey, partner! How ya feelin' today?" AC's voice rang out. He flashed a bright smile that melted Lisa instantly where she sat. A gasp caught in her throat. *Maybe this is why he has kept it hidden. That smile is surely a dangerous weapon.*

AC chose not to notice that Lisa had been feeding Matty, commenting instead that the boy seemed to be looking better. "No rough housing, tho, I expect, for awhile, anyway."

"Mr. Greening, whatever happened to your mustache?" Lisa asked in amazement.

" Yea, what happened to you?" Matthew asked incredulously.

"Becky didn't take to it," he stated. AC had actually gotten somewhat used to seeing himself without the mustache for the last day, even though he did feel rather naked without it. He had brushed several sweet kisses across Becky's cheek, which more than made up for his self-consciousness.

Lisa hesitated a moment, so as to absorb what she was hearing. "Are you saying that Becky didn't like your mustache... and so you shaved it off?" she asked incredulously.

"My mama always taught me to aim to please my house guests," he retorted.

"I can't believe you!" Lisa chided. She had become fond of the mustache, even though it often kept her from reading his expressions.

"It'll grow back." AC said, and his glance silenced further comments.

What kind of a man do we have here, Lisa? This is certainly one of a kind.

Lisa watched in awe as AC unloaded the bags at the foot of her son's bed. Matthew's eyes grew wide as each article of western wear was pulled from the wrappings. The youngster was clearly in ecstasy, and it was difficult to hide her own excitement at this favor showered on the aspiring cowboy, even though she was dead set against the cowboy part. She hoped the phase would pass quickly.

"Here's your coffee, Lisa honey." The voice behind AC was too loud and cheery and sent a cold shiver down AC's back. He turned to see Brent, smiling broadly, carrying two steaming Styrofoam cups. The business suit clad man walked past AC acknowledging him only with a sidelong glance.

AC felt betrayed. Why did she allow this jerk to offer comfort when she had refused AC'S? Brent didn't give a hoot about Matty, couldn't she see that? Fury blazed within him. Lisa was thinking only of herself and not the boy. And who did Brent think he was butting in, claiming her boldly in front of him with touches, glances, smiles and smoothness? That slick city boy didn't really care about this hurting woman or her children. Well, maybe the woman, but certainly not her cute kids. Would this fancy guy have done something so foolish as to shave his hair off for the sweet little bit of a girl with big brown eyes waiting for her mother and brother at the ranch this very moment? Yet he had done it without a second thought. OK, he did have a second thought when gazing in the morning mirror at the strikingly bare lip. But he would do it again in a heartbeat for those innocent brown eyes.

Maybe that was it. Maybe he was thinking too much with the beating of his heart and not enough with his common sense. Of course this successful businessman would sweep this young widow off her feet with his fancy flashy ways. Yet, he was a businessman too. It took careful planning and business sense to manage a cow-calf operation successfully, especially these past couple of years. And AC had done a good job of it. He was solvent and proud of it. Lisa's uneasy voice brought AC to the moment.

"Mr. Greening, you remember.... Brent."

"I do, ma'am," the tall cowboy tipped his hat to Lisa, and shot Brent a sharp look that he hoped would burn a hole through him. Brent clearly had a hold of Lisa, but now was not the time to confront him about it. His concern had to be Matty now. "Well, I see you've got all the help you need here ma'am," the stiff reply was tight, yet even. "I'd best be heading back to the ranch" AC strode over to Matty' bedside and met the boy's eyes with kindness and affection. "You keep on healing, OK? You're gonna be fine. I'll tell your brothers and sister 'hey' for you." He patted Matty's shoulder with big calloused hands and winked.

"Thanks, AC." the boy beamed.

"Yes, thank you so much... for everything." Lisa's comment seemed genuine.

"No problem."

Glaring at Brent before tipping his hat to Lisa, he said no more.

13

After a long morning of waiting for the doctor to make his rounds, Matty and Lisa were finally given permission for discharge with strict instructions for very limited activity. Lisa knew it would be a major problem for her to keep her highly active pre- teen calm, but she hoped she would figure something out. She had to.

Lisa was in the middle of helping Matty get dressed and his things together when she remembered about the bill. Ugh. The bill for the past five days in the hospital and all of the tests was more than she dared think about right now. When the nurse came in with the discharge papers, Lisa spoke up weakly. "I need to speak with someone in the billing department about working out a payment plan," she reminded the nurse.

"Oh, the bill has been taken care of, Mrs. Taff... I presumed you knew," the nurse shot a questioning glance at Lisa, and proceeded with the oral discharge instructions.

Now how did the bill get taken care of already? And why would she presume I knew?

AC entered the room as the nurse finished her instructions and motioned Lisa to sign the papers she held out. She had asked AC to drive them back to Alpine, despite Brent's vehement opposition. Her car and children were there, after all, and she needed to thank Emma personally for her attentiveness to her other children the past several days. Mechanically, Lisa signed the papers, her mind still reeling from the nurse's revelation. Matthew submitted to being wheeled in a wheelchair to AC's waiting truck. He slid into the middle of the front seat of the quad cab. Lisa got in beside him, and AC strode to the driver's side. As they rolled out of the hospital parking lot, she drew Matthew close and reveled in his presence beside her.

***

AC pushed away from the table as he offered his thanks to Emma for another delicious breakfast. Hobbie was close on his heels. "Jimmy Joe and I will go work on that fence today, Hobbie, would you see what you can do with that blasted generator? I'm thinkin' that we may have to switch over to total solar for awhile and overhaul that contraption," AC tried to hide his concern.

"I thought we were fixin' to get that new one you've been sockin' away funds for here pretty quick." Hobbie said, confusion evident in his face.

AC was always straight with his foreman. "I had cause to dip into the funds," he said quietly.

Hobbie gave a quick nod. "I'll see what I can do," he replied as he slumped down the short path to the generator shed.

14

Lisa opened the door to the gallery on the main street of Alpine. It had been months since Matthew's accident, and she had given reluctant permission for him to ride the gentlest horse on the ranch this morning. The other children were at the library for Rita's story hour. This was her chance to talk with Brent. A gentle tinkle announced her presence. Brent looked up from behind the counter and smiled. Lisa felt her resolve begin to dwindle, but she inhaled deeply through her nose and exhaled through her mouth, a trick she had learned in the natural childbirth classes she had gone to with Grant. Grant... she strengthened at the mere thought of him and the uttering of his name under her breath.

Brent walked quickly and smoothly toward Lisa, he seemed eager to have her in his embrace. Although their relationship had been strained lately, he probably felt sure he could recover any territory that had been lost. Reaching to gather her in his arms, he planted a kiss on her cheek. Immediately she stiffened and stepped back.

Lisa stepped toward the glass counter containing expensive jewelry and turned toward it. Not wanting to be backed up against it, she pretended to look at the top row of silver and turquoise. The businessman scooted close to her, still keeping his arm around the slender shoulder.

"I need to talk to you, Brent," she stepped to the side and out of the man's reach.

He followed her, "Sure... how about lunch? It is rather slow right now, anyway."

"No, thank you, Brent...I just came to tell you... well... that I need to end our relationship... as anything other than just platonic friends, and, well business associates for Grant's works... and..."

"Grant...Grant! Grant is gone, Lisa, GONE! But you are still so filled with him that you can't have a decent relationship with anyone else! Grant is not coming back!"

"You are exactly right. I am full of Grant. My life is filled with what Grant left behind... five beautiful children. They are what I have left of him and I am responsible for them now... for their happiness and ours as a family. They are my life right now, Brent, and I'm going to live it...my life... with them." She felt strangely weak and strong simultaneously. She set her chin and blinked furiously as she met Brent's steely gaze.

Brent finally looked away and retreated behind the glass counter. He leaned on it and faced her once again. All kindness and emotion was gone. The tone was flat, "Our association is over. When the paintings sell, I'll send you the profit less my commission. That's the agreement we had at the beginning. You can see yourself out." The slender gallery owner turned abruptly and busied himself with paperwork.

Have I done the right thing? He has been a friend to me and the children. Warm tears rushed down as she fled from the shop before she broke into sobs. Somewhere deep inside, Lisa knew she had done the right thing. The right thing just wasn't very easy this time. A quick glance at her wristwatch revealed that the children would be at story time at the library with Rita for another 45 minutes. She would have time to collect herself before picking them up.

Lisa quickly turned the key in the ignition and followed the back roads to the cabin. A familiar vehicle sat parked intrusively in the circular gravel driveway. It was just what she didn't need right now.

Why was he always showing up in her life when she was the most vulnerable? He, with those penetrating eyes that seemed to be able to see deep into her soul, and his uncanny understanding of where she was emotionally. Such a steadying touch that she had felt once and rejected. Why was he always there, complicating life? And who did he think he was, anyway, being in her house when she was not at home? He certainly was audacious.

"Hi, Mama," Matthew called from the couch, where he sat with AC, holding a large glass of something over ice.

AC immediately rose and removed his hat, holding it loosely in one hand. "Howdy, ma'am. Matty was real hospitable in invitin' me in for a glass of...juice, I guess it is. How's your day goin'?" Bright blue eyes pierced her pain.

"Mama?" she shot a questioning glare at Matthew.

"Yea, that is what AC calls his mom, he calls her Mama. How about that?" Matthew smiled broadly.

"Yes, well, I prefer just Mom, thank you. And as for my day, it has been the pits, actually. I've just lost my best friend," she snapped, "Would you like to gloat?" She strode past them and set her purse on the far coffee table.

AC winked at Matty, but did not miss a beat with his calm response. "Some days are like that, I reckon, ma'am. Lord knows we all have them. I'm sure sorry today had to be one of them for you."

That voice was so soft and soothing!

The tall cowboy continued, "Matty, I sure do appreciate you inviting me in to sit awhile and thanks for the juice and all. You did your mama proud. And thanks for riding with me this mornin'. We couldn't have pushed those heifers without you. You did a good job." He winked at Matty and addressed himself to Lisa this time, "Ma'am, I sure am obliged to you for loaning me Matthew this morning." He strode to the door, spurs jingling. "See you, Matty...Lisa." Opening the door, he jammed on the Stetson.

Suddenly Lisa spun around and stepped to the door. "I'm sorry, Mr. Greening," she said softly, "I shouldn't have been so short with you." For a brief moment, she allowed her eyes to meet his.

"No harm done," his voice washed over her like a warm wave and his eyes betrayed what his regrown mustache hid. Tentatively he touched her shoulder. "I never have been good at figurin' relationships, but maybe you didn't lose your best friend... maybe you just found yourself."

Before the impact of the words hit Lisa, AC had tipped his hat and was gone.

15

"Hello?" Emma answered the phone.

"Hi, Emma? This is Lisa Taff... I was trying to reach Mr. Greening... uh, AC, is he around?" There was an excitement in her voice that Emma could not escape noticing.

"Why sure, honey, just a minute. He's on the porch." Emma handed the cell phone to AC, who was pouring over the books, looking for a few lost dollars. She forgot to advise him who was calling, and he spoke gruffly, still thinking of the missing dollars,

"This is AC."

"Hi...AC, I just called because I got a teaching position... and I was so excited...I just had to tell someone," she suddenly felt silly and embarrassed that she would even have thought to call him. There was silence on the other end of the line, so she continued. "It is a good position with the University of Phoenix... I can conduct the class via the Internet. The University is going to set me up with a computer and web cam here at home, and I will go to Phoenix once a month for an all day class on Saturday." She paused to another short silence and continued, "I was just so excited when I dialed the phone ...but... now it seems so silly... that I called, and..." she let her voice trail off, her momentum wearing thin.

It took AC a moment to get his mind off the books and to realize the opportunity of this moment. He had only seen Lisa and her family a few times since Matthew's accident. She had only allowed Matthew to return to riding with him a few times, and AC missed the boy fiercely. He had convinced her to visit on several occasions, under the guise of having a picnic, or a celebration for Hobbie's birthday, but the truth was that his heart ached for Lisa and her children.

"Not at all, Lisa," the tenderness in his voice wrapped around her, warming her to the core. It was the first time he had called her anything but ma'am or Mrs. Taff. She felt strangely affirmed.

"This calls for a celebration," Lisa could feel his grin through the phone lines, as he said quickly. "How about dinner Saturday at Bear Wallow?"

"Well...yes...sure, I'll have to get a sitter," she announced.

"Why?" he responded, "Are the kids sick or something?"

"I just... well... I didn't know that they were included in the invitation."

"Oh, ... if you would rather not have them along.."

"No!" Lisa interrupted, "It's not that at all. It's just that not too many people invite me out to dinner meaning to feed my whole crew, too," she chuckled.

"Well, I do, Lisa." He had spoken her name twice in the last few minutes, never having realized before how nice it sounded; how good it felt rolling over his tongue.

"OK, that sounds wonderful. Thank you, AC."

"It is a deal, then. I'll be by your house about 6:00."

Long after Lisa hung up the phone, she felt the warmth in AC's voice and continued her wonderment of how a man like AC could simply take her and her children under his wing so completely. It scared her for a moment, but by the time Lisa closed the house down for the night, a strange sense of peace flooded her.

Bear Wallow buzzed as usual on Saturday night, and the party of 7 in the back room was no exception. The children were filled with anticipation of the new school year, only a few weeks away, and all of them chattered excitedly, all except for Matty. He had again slumped into a behavior pattern that threatened to send Lisa into a tailspin. When talk of the ranch came up, his face brightened and Lisa recognized that her fear that he was missing his time at the ranch must be true. The last time he was allowed to come to the ranch was just after his colt was born. Matty had named him Grease, because AC had pointed out that even on his knobby legs, the colt fairly flew around the corrals like "greased lightning". Matty had thought about Lightning for a name, but had decided Grease was more unique.

Lisa sat with her napkin folded in her lap, encouraging the boys to finish their plates. The realization suddenly struck her that this seemed more like a family dinner than a celebratory dinner out with a friend. It surprised her how easily that thought came to mind, but she was not willing to let it settle within her.

AC lingered at the house after several videos were watched and the children tucked into bed for the night. It seemed that he did not want to leave. Did he want to savor the moment as long as she did? Tonight had felt good. Very good.

He ventured to put his arm around Lisa as they sat on the couch. She quickly asked if he wanted a drink and jumped up to retrieve two glasses of iced tea from the refrigerator. AC remained undaunted. He came up beside her as she stood at the sink. Slipping an arm around her shoulder, he drew her closer and she did not pull away this time.

"I have an idea," he said softly.

Lisa's eyes widened and her heart pounded faster than the already rapid pace it had jumped to moments before. "Oh?" She squeaked out.

"Yea... I was noticing that..." he turned to face her, standing close, looking into her sea-green eyes, "That Matty seems a little nervous about school starting up again."

Lisa let out the breath she realized she had been holding with definite relief.

"And I have a proposition to make," AC continued. He still stood close, and looked earnestly into her eyes. "How about if you let Matty come to the ranch and stay with me Monday thru Thursday and go to the little one room school house down on the Blue. It's a fine little school, and the teacher is mighty good. And the kids, well, they're just good kids. Jimmy Joe's kids go there...and he could be around the animals, which seems to settle him, and I could bring him back up here for Thursday night through Sunday afternoon." He was determined to make his whole presentation before she had time to protest. "I think it would be good for him, and of course I could help him with his studyin'. Me, and also Emma and Hobbie, I mean. I think it would be good for him," he repeated, not willing to admit that it would be good for him, too.

Lisa stepped back. "You want me to send Matty away??" she asked in disbelief.

"No...No... just share him," AC stammered. "I'm sorry," he said seeing the alarm in her face, "I'm sorry, Lisa. That was a bad idea. This evening has just set me all a fluster, and I don't even know what I'm sayin'." He turned away from her, one hand on his hip, the other running through his blonde hair, wondering how to make things right. The company of a beautiful woman and cheerful children this evening had felt so good. "It is just that tonight felt so good, and it lifted my heart considerably. I just know that he has a hard time of school and all, and he's still kind of a hurtin' little boy, and I was just trying to help him... I was trying to help... you..." he sighed and dropped his arms to his side. He turned to face her again. "I was out of line, Lisa," he looked deep into her eyes, clouded with tears, "Please forgive me."

"Oh... I'm the one with the advanced Psychology degree, and I don't even know how to help my own son, Arlow," she dropped her head and he pulled her against his muscled chest. He stroked her hair and back for a long time, letting her cry into the part of him that housed his heart. He noticed she had used his given name.

16

AC walked up beside Matty, who was perched on the corral fence, watching the young colt that belonged to him.

"He's fine, isn't he?" AC nodded his head toward mother and foal.

"He sure is, AC, and I bet he's smart, too. I bet he'll be real easy to train." Matty was energetic.

AC stretched his arm around the young boy's shoulder as he swung up beside him. They sat silently for a long while, drinking up the cool sunshine and crisp air.

"Speakin' of bein' smart, Matty, how about you? You ever think about what you might want to do when you grow up?" AC avoided Matty's eyes, looking instead at the horizon, past the horses and corrals.

"Well," Matthew hesitated, "Mom says I have to go to college. I think she wants me to be something big, like a doctor or something."

"Hmm...That is mighty big. What do you want to be?"

"I really like animals, and being around here and the horses and stuff. I think I'd like to be a rancher... like you." Matty dropped his gaze to his boots, "Or an artist... like my dad."

AC hugged the thin shoulders silently.

"My mom wants me to make something of my life, not just waste it wandering around the countryside. Maybe I should be a veterinarian. That way I could be a doctor and work with the animals too." The voice was small and uncertain.

"Hey, that would be good. Then I could have a resident vet on the place." AC's eyes twinkled as he smiled genuinely at the boy.

Matty's face brightened. "Do ranchers really hire resident vets?"

"I would," AC winked, "If I found the right one." He tousled the pile of dark brown hair and jumped off the corral fence and turned to extend a hand to the aspiring vet.

"We'd better get you on home."

A car pulled out of the circular driveway of Matthew's house as AC pulled in.

"Looks like you missed out on company," AC frowned at Matty.

"I'm glad I missed him. That's Mr. Brent's car."

"Oh?"

"Yeah, he and mom were mad at each other, but they made some kind of agreement to be just friends. Anyway, she's not marrying him yet, and that's good. He came over today to get Mom's new "technology" all set up for her."

"I thought she got it last week"

"She did. She got it put together and everything, but Mr. Brent doesn't think that she can do a thing without him." Matty sighed, put his hand on his chest and batted his eyes.

They busted into laughter before going into the house.

"Hi Mom, I'm home!" Matty yelled as he closed the door behind AC.

"In here," Lisa's voice rang out from another room.

A small room just off the living room had been newly converted to an office. Matty took off in the direction of the kitchen, while AC stepped into the doorway of the office.

"Well, it looks like your friend got you set up just right," AC took off his gray felt hat and ran his fingers through his thick blonde hair. It was slightly greasy and stayed in place.

"Yes... well... Brent did help me get it all in place. He knows his way around computers and technology in general very well. He has several of Grant's paintings in his Internet gallery," Lisa continued typing as she spoke.

Matty returned to the office, handing AC a cold glass of lemonade.

Lisa continued her praise, "Brent is going to help me set up a chat room for my students, too. I'll host it one night a week, and they can take turns hosting the other days."

She closed the program and turned to the two who held cold drinks in their hands. She looked at Matty with a raised eyebrow, "You didn't bring me a glass?" She frowned at

Matthew this time, and her kidding turned serious, "And take those things off your boots, young man," she cast a disapproving look at both Matthew and AC. Matthew scurried back to the entryway and removed his boots.

"Why do you always wear those things on the back of your boots, anyway? Is there a point to wearing them, besides making noise and scratching up the floor?" Lisa asked.

"They're called spurs, and they don't even touch the floor, ma'am," AC defended, "A good cowboy knows how to use his spur to gently guide his horse to do what needs to be done. Sometimes a ranch horse can be a mite stubborn."

"Well, I don't allow Matthew to wear them in the house." Lisa stated, "They will mark the furniture."

"I'll stay away from your furniture," AC retorted. He followed Lisa as she swept past them toward the kitchen.

"Is Brent going to take you down to Phoenix to help you find your way around there too? You know, to make sure you don't get lost or anything?" AC pressed.

The sarcasm in his voice irritated her. "Mr. Greening," she huffed, "I am not some weak and timid little woman who cannot think for herself, and needs to be led around."

"There's some who think you are," AC replied.

"And what do you think?" She almost whispered. *Here it comes, Lisa, and you asked for every bit of it.*

The minute dragged on before the gentle voice stated simply, "I think you're a mighty strong woman. And smart too, and you don't need a man just bein' around touchin' on you.

You need more than a man to just hang your arm on." *And I'm that man.*

"And of course you are an expert on what I need and don't need." her eyes threw sparks in AC's direction.

"No, not an expert, Mrs. Taff. I just think you are doin' a fine job here with your kids."

"Hopefully this job will open up a way for us to get back to a more civilized area."

"I thought you liked Alpine."

"Its alright for now, but this was Grant's dream... not mine," a hint of sadness in her voice.

"And you think it's a bad dream?"

"Don't you see? I want my children to make something out of themselves... to be "somebodies". There's a big wide world of opportunity out there for them. I want more for them, and Matthew in particular, than all this cowboy thing. I want him growing up knowing how to speak proper English and get along in the world. It is competitive out there, and I don't want Matthew dropping all the endings off of his words, and walking around in tight jeans and pointy boots that rattle, tipping his hat all the time, and spitting chewing tobacco!"

"I don't dip!"

"Oh, don't take it personally, Mr. Greening, I just want good solid opportunities for Matthew. He needs to grow up and stop playing cowboy!"

"Is that what you think ranchin' is... PLAYING cowboy? I get up before daylight and work hard all day and sometimes all night. It is an everyday job, and I don't get any vacations. Running a ranch is a business, ma'am, just like that high faloutin' boyfriend of yours runnin' that art shop... only I don't get to strut around in fancy clothes and eat lunch out at the café every day. I run a ranching_*business* and I'm *good* at it. I run 950 head of cattle here, and I have a share of another 900 in Wyoming. I can break horses and train horses, and get the best out of every square inch of land that I own." AC could feel the color rising in his cheeks, but he would not back down on this one, not even for Lisa.

"Every ranch I've ever operated, I've run it mostly in the black. I've made a profit almost every year. Oh, I'll allow most times the profit hasn't been real big, but I've eaten and kept me and my help fed and clothed, my cattle and horses healthy, my bank note paid, and my equipment runnin'. I don't guess I can ask more of the good Lord than that. No, ma'am, it may not be a glamorous job, but I enjoy it. That's nothing to sniff at. There's worse things in the world than runnin' an honest hard workin' business."

AC jammed on his hat and set the glass in his hand down on the counter a little too forcefully. "Thank you for the lemonade." Spurs jingled as he stomped through the kitchen and toward the front door. "And I think the mustache is just fine!"

"Who said anything about your mustache?" Lisa retorted.

"You were fixin' to!" He slammed the door behind him.

17

"You mean you're leavin'? Just like that?" AC could not believe Lisa's voice on the other end of the phone. He sat at his desk on the porch in the twilight.

"Well, yea," the she replied.

AC could almost see the excitement in her voice.

" I finally found a school that I think Matty will be happy in. It's a school for gifted and talented that will really challenge him and Brent helped me work out an apartment. I know it seems rather sudden, but everything is just falling into place, all the opportunities, the furnished apartment, the new and better contract with the College..."

"I thought that the teaching job was one that you could do by the computer and just go down to Phoenix once every month or two." AC tried to sound casual, but his insides were churning. He tried to keep his voice at an even keel.

"The Administration at the Thunderbird Campus didn't think it was working out quite like we first expected. It's a probationary position for the first year, and then we'll re-evaluate the situation and go from there."

"Hmm," he mused.

"I thought you'd be happy for us... especially for Matty... that he'll be able to find his niche..."

"His niche... or yours?"

"This opportunity to actually teach at the West Campus could lead to a professorship at the main University," she obviously ignored his question.

"Is this really what you want?" AC hoped the devastation that had just been wrecked was not clearly evident in his voice.

"AC, this is a golden opportunity that has just been set before us all. You, yourself, said several weeks ago that Matty seemed nervous about starting school again. We toured the school yesterday. Matty spent the afternoon with the class he would be in, and loved it."

"He wants to go?" AC asked, a hint of sadness in his voice.

18

The next days slid together like a blur. AC needed to spend as much time as possible with Matty and his family. He would miss the boy ... the whole family. But if that was truly what was best for them, he had no choice but to watch them go, even though his heart felt like it had been ripped from his body and lay in the harsh Arizona sun.

Matty seemed happy and excited. The other children seemed happy, and most of all, Lisa appeared happy and positive about it all. AC had never seen her quite so exuberant.

They left amid hugs and promises to write, call and visit. Lisa left the house in tact for now, said she had no intention of selling it, and they pledged to return for visits often, spending vacations in Alpine. The schools that the children were enrolled in had year round schedules, and every three months they would have a month off. Matthew had consoled AC with the fact that his mom had promised to let him return and spend most, if not all, of his vacation time at the Ranch.

It didn't seem to be much of a big deal to anyone else, but AC silently wondered if this was the beginning of the end of his relationship with Matthew, his family, and his mother.

Maybe he had been wrong in his thoughts of building a relationship with Matthew, the others and Lisa. Maybe he was no better than Brent, and had just been acting out of his own selfish desire for family and the heart of a beautiful woman. Was he that far off in his spiritual walk that he had let his own ways cloud him into thinking he was following a higher purpose?

Doubts gnawed at his mind and heart as he stumbled through the days and weeks that followed.

He missed Matthew, but he found himself thinking more and more about Lisa. Had he really just used Matty to get close to Lisa? His thoughts tormented him day and night and he wondered if the last year and a half had been a lie.

19

"Hello," AC held the cell phone loosely to his right ear. He stepped a little further out into the parking lot of Diamond Feed Store, until the crackling in his ear disappeared.

"Hello?" he repeated.

" Hi... A.C.?"

"Hey... is that you Matty?"

"Yea... what are you up to?"

"Oh, I'm just here in town pickin' up some feed. Hobbie's got a couple of projects goin' at the Ranch, so I had to come by myself today. I'm just fixin' to go grab a steak before headin' back. How are you doin'?" He suddenly felt like he had been rambling, but it was good to hear the boy's voice.

"Uh... um... I'm OK... uh... you say you're in Springerville?"

"Yep."

"Uh... I'm in Show Low!...AC, do you think you could come and get me?"

"Well, Matty, What on earth are you doin' in Show Low?"

"I'm just here at the hospital..."

"At the hospital! What's wrong? ... Who's sick? Is your mom all right?"

"Nobody is sick, AC. This is just where I told Todd's dad to drop me off. This is the only place around here that I know."

"Now, back up just a minute, Matty. Tell me who Todd's dad is, and who Todd is, and why you are at the hospital in Show Low if you aren't sick!" AC tried to keep his composure in the midst of the confusion swirling in his mind.

"It's kind of a long story," Matty replied sheepishly.

"Does your Momma know where you are?" AC quizzed. The silence on the other end of the line was his answer. "Come on, son, tell me what's goin' on."

"Jake and I kinda got into it with Brent... and he jerked us around..."

"Brent is down there? And what do you mean, jerked you around?"

"Well... you know..."

"No, I don't."

"Well, he has been hanging around a lot. He has an apartment down here, and we kind of got into an argument...he said we were sassing him, and he roughed us up a little."

"Did he hit you?" AC interrupted.

"Not really. He was kind of shoving us around. I fell into the side of the doorway, and when I fell I knocked Jacob into the end table. We were taking him on together. Jake has a cut on his eyebrow, and my cheek just smarts a little. He said we ought to just high tail it out of there if we knew what was good for us... so I did. I left."

" And Jacob?"

"He stayed."

"And where was your mom in all this?" AC tried to sound calm, even as his blood coursed feverishly through his veins.

"She's been pretty busy... She was at her class."

"And what was he doing there without your mom being there?"

"It's a long story, AC. He left. The sitter came, and I left."

"Do you think your mom is home now and will be worried about you? And how did you get to Show Low?" The questions whizzed through AC's mind.

"I told you, I got a ride from Todd's dad," Matty seemed a bit irritated.

"I suppose Todd is a friend of yours?" AC struggled to put the pieces together.

"Yea, kind of, I guess he is the closest thing to a friend I have down here."

"Why would his dad give you a ride to run away? Matty, your mom's probably worried sick."

"Oh no, she thinks I'm spending the night with Todd. And people in the school are kind of free thinkers...I just said the right words the way they needed to hear them...AC, will you come and get me...please?" Suddenly his voice sounded weak and vulnerable...pleading.

AC tried to collect his thoughts. "I'm comin' to Show Low, Matty, it will take me around 45 minutes."

"Thanks, AC."

"You do know, Matthew, that one of us needs to call your mom and tell her about this."

There was silence.

"Matthew, are you there?" AC questioned.

"Yes," Matthew replied softly.

"Well?"

"Do you want to?" Matthew's question was more like a plea.

Suddenly AC's mind flashed to a time when Clay had whipped him for leaving a gate open in the hay barn. His horse had gotten into the hay and gorged himself on the hay. The horse bloated and died. A cold shiver jerked him back to the present. "No, I don't want to... but I will."

"OK"

"Do you have any money?"

"Yea, I have 10 dollars," Matthew sounded like he felt he was rich.

"Listen to me, Matthew, you go across the street to the Wal Mart and get something to eat... no, stay there at the hospital and get something to eat, and then...I don't think you should just be wandering around there. Uh, I know Kathy White. She's in the hospital business office, on the first floor by the main entrance. Do you think you can find the business office and tell her I said for you to wait there for me? You wait right there for me, you hear?"

"Yea, I kinda know my way around here. I've been here before, remember?"

"I remember."

20

Lisa kicked her shoes off and plopped on the couch. She was tempted to let the machine pick up, but she finally reached out and picked up the receiver.

"Hello."

"Hello, Lisa? This is AC Greening."

"Hello, AC, how are you?" her voice was sweet and a little dreamy.

"Well, I'm tryin' to figure that out right now, ma'am."

"Oh?"

"I just got a call on my cell phone from Matty. He's at the hospital in Show Low."

"He's what?" She shot off the couch and was immediately at the front window; as if by looking out she would see Matty. "What's going on...why is he at the hospital in Show Low? Tell me."

"Seems he ran away. He said he's not hurt, not physically at least. He got a ride up there with a friend he was supposed to be spending the night with."

"With Todd?"

"Well, I guess with Todd and his daddy."

AC's voice had a strange strain to it. It almost sounded like he was choking up...or holding something back. "Well, I'm glad he ran to you," Lisa was relieved. "He has talked of running away so many times...I didn't think he would ever do it. I suppose that now that he has someone to run to, he got up the courage to try it."

"And that's OK with you?"

"No, running away isn't OK with me, Mr. Greening, but I'm glad that he had you to run to." His naiveté was starting to get on her nerves. "I'll run up to Show Low and pick him up. I don't even know how long it takes to get to Show Low... Did you tell him to stay at the hospital?"

"I told him I would come and get him. I'm on my way right now. I'll be there in about 45 minutes." his voice was cold and stony.

"Oh...OK... well, were you planning on bringing him down here? I'm sure he will appreciate getting to spend some time with you, or I can meet you half way or something." She tried to apologize for the inconvenience she knew this out- of-the -way trip must be to him.

"You don't have to sacrifice your kids, Lisa, to get your needs met," AC blurted out.

"I beg your pardon?" Lisa's irritation was starting to show, "What are you talking about?"

"You don't have to sacrifice your family to get your needs met," he repeated.

"And what does a cowboy know about getting needs met? Isn't that vocabulary a little out of your world?"

82

"You're not the only one who can read a Psychology book. I do know how to read, you know."

Lisa sensed his sarcasm. "Since when have you started reading Psychology?"

"Since I met you."

"Oh, and you think I am sacrificing my children in exchange for self-gratification? What on earth are you talking about?"

"Matty ran away, didn't he?"

"Matty is thirteen! Thirteen year olds do crazy things- they are adolescents!"

"Did you talk to Jacob?"

"No... I just got home. What does he have to do with Matthew running?"

"Talk to him. I'll call you back when I get to Show Low."

The receiver clicked and she was again alone in the room.

21

AC sat across the square table from Matthew in the Wal Mart snack bar. Both sipped blue ICEEs. AC snuck another glance at the red and swollen cheek of the young boy. Matty had winced earlier, when AC had reached to touch it lightly with the back of his finger. He knew the time had come to return the call to Lisa. He was uncertain of how that would go, since his insides felt both like melting and exploding. He had given his word to Matty that something would change, and begged the Lord to use him as an instrument of that change, but just how it would all turn out, he had no clue. He did know that it would involve putting some hard questions to Lisa.

Once they returned to his pick-up, AC slowly dialed Lisa's number. The answering machine came on after the second ring. He started to leave a message.

"Hello, Mr. Greening," Lisa's voice was noticeably shaky.

"Hi... I've got Matthew. He's doin' OK for the moment. We'll head that way... I think we need to talk."

"That won't be necessary," Lisa interrupted.

"I think it *is* necessary. We need to talk, ma'am," AC wasn't going to budge on this.

"It isn't necessary to come down here. I'm packed. All I have to do is load the car. We are ready to leave."

AC could hear the strain in her voice. She sounded broken. "Alright, ma'am, but Matty mentioned that there are some things from his room that he would like to have." He was still angry with her, but the sound of her voice gripped his heart.

"All of his things are in a box. It is all boxed up, and we are ready to go," she insisted.

AC recalled the small U-Haul trailer that Brent had pulled when they had left Alpine four months ago. "I have my pick-up, Lisa, do you need me to haul those boxes for you?"

"Oh... yeah, I suppose so... there are about 15 of them." She sounded as though she had not thought of how she might fit the boxes into her mini-van.

Without thinking things through thoroughly, AC found himself saying, "Hobbie says it will take me about 3 hours to get to Phoenix. Will that be alright?"

"Yes."

"Can you wait that long?"

"Yes."

He wished he could reach through the phone and touch her...reassure her, but he merely said, "Hang in there with the Lord...We'll see you soon." Somehow he felt as if time was of the essence, as they sped down the highway in the early afternoon sunshine.

22

AC's hands gripped the steering wheel tightly as the traffic around him picked up. What ever had made him volunteer to come to the insane city of Phoenix? Hobbie had always been good about driving in major cities. It just wasn't in AC's constitution to deal with the insanity of heavy traffic and city culture. Sweat suddenly poured down his face as he ambled slowly down the freeway into the outskirts of Phoenix.

"Everybody's passing us," Matty noted.

"I can see that," AC muttered. He was using too much energy concentrating on his driving to speak very much.

"The speed limit is still 65," Matthew stated, with a glance in AC's direction.

"I reckon if they all want to go that fast... they can just go around me." He liked it right there in the right lane. He wanted to wipe the sweat from his forehead and mustache, but he knew he could not let go of the wheel. Not even with one hand. Instead he let the liquid run into his mouth, tasting the saltiness of it.

"My dad got a ticket on the interstate once for going too slow," Matthew checked his wide grin quickly, and returned his gaze sheepishly to the road in front of him. "He was looking for a good picture," he said softly.

"It's OK, son, you just be sure to tell me where to go...y'hear?"

Matty's face brightened again. "OK."

Several miles on, AC could feel the sweat leaving small trails down his back and chest. It annoyed him to no end, but he kept focused on the road.

Matthew broke the silence again, "I think you should move into the middle lane."

"I'm fine right here."

"No, you need to merge left," Matty insisted.

"Why?"

"Because this lane exits right up here."

"Well how did I get in it?"

"The lane we are in just turned into an exit only."

AC mumbled under his breath as he turned on his left blinker and attempted to steer the truck into the nearly bumper-to-bumper traffic. The tires made a thunderous rumbling on the pavement separating the traffic lanes from the exit lane, as he swerved into the flow of traffic and narrowly escaped taking the exit.

Matty loosened his death grip on the door handle. "It isn't too much further," he offered, "The sign said Thunderbird two and three-fourths miles."

"OK... you just watch and tell me where to veer off."

The 2 3/4 miles seemed more like 100, as cars merged into and out of the right lane where AC drove. Once they had exited the freeway, he was not as relieved as he thought he would be. They traveled down the equally busy Thunderbird Avenue, this time with the added excitement of traffic lights.

"How far?" AC grunted after the fourth traffic light. His knuckles were now permanently white, and his hands felt molded to the steering wheel.

"Not far," Matty replied cheerfully.

After two more lights, AC queried, "Are we talkin' miles...or blocks?"

"I think miles."

"Humph...let's get 'er done then," He glanced over at Matty, who gave him a thumbs-up.

23

Hang in there with the Lord. Hang in there with the Lord?? How could she do that? She had totally destroyed her life and her children's lives. She had let Grant down, and God down, and made a general mess of the whole situation. She had turned her back on the people who had really been helping her and her family all along. She hugged Becky and the younger boys close while Jacob sulked at the other end of the small living room, a small cut on his left eyebrow. She had tried to doctor it for him, but he would not let her. She now wondered if she had lost both older boys for good. Fresh tears welled and fell.

The knock on the door made her jump. There were no lights on in the apartment, and the curtains were closed. She crept silently to the door to look out the peephole. What she saw flooded her with fear as well as delight.

AC stood with his hat in his hand, his gray cotton shirt obviously soaked. Matty stood at his side, small and frail, a red welt on his left cheek. Lisa removed the chain from the door, unlocked the deadbolt and the door, and held it open. She stepped past the tall cowboy and clutched Matthew tightly to her. He drew back suddenly, turning his left cheek away from her embrace. She hugged him close, sobs overcoming her in a familiar wave. "I'm so sorry," she managed to whisper as she led them into the apartment.

The children were frozen in terror on the couch. Becky raised a small hand in a slight wave for a brief moment. AC Looked at Jacob in the easy chair and flashed a fierce gaze at Lisa. She dodged his gaze, and kept her eyes on the floor, as the boys and AC loaded their boxes of belongings in the back of AC's truck in relative silence. Lisa had already packed their suitcases in the van and quietly led the children to the waiting vehicle.

AC picked up Becky on the way.

"Hi, sweetie," he said gently.

"Hi." Becky whispered, as she cautiously hugged his neck. The sweat didn't seem to bother her as she finally snuggled her forehead into his neck muscles.

"I missed you," Lisa heard Becky say before AC set her in the car. She noticed that Becky did not protest the brush of AC's mustached kiss on her forehead. He tousled the hair of the other boys.

"I'll follow you," he said simply, before striding back to the truck where Matthew and Jacob both waited for him.

Her chest tightened, and Lisa could hardly breathe as she led the way out of Phoenix through the grueling rush hour traffic. She kept an eye in the rear view mirror for the gray Silverado and wondered how she would ever stay on the road between the sobs.

She was grateful for the children's quietness. She suspected they were shocked and disturbed by her uncontrolled weeping, but she could not for the life of her bring her tangled emotions under submission.

As they snaked their way at last through the Salt River Canyon, thoughts of tumbling to the bottom of the Canyon raced through Lisa's mind. It was certainly possible. All it would take would be one small swerve on the narrow road. One slight turn of the wheel would send her off the narrow road, into the feeble guardrail, that protected only inches of ground, before careening to the depths of a mental, emotional and physical rest she so longed for. Many a traveler had been sent to a final peace on this highway. It was widely known for being one of the most scenic ... and deadly stretches of road.

"Are we almost there?" Peter's small voice pierced Lisa's thoughts and heart. "I'm hungry."

She looked in the side mirror to see 2 headlights following closely.

"Almost," she said weakly, and turned on the radio to chase all thoughts out of her jumbled mind. "We'll get something to eat soon," she assured Peter.

Wave after wave of despair and hopelessness overcame her as she pressed on through the evening twilight. She had to get back to Alpine...back to Grant. She had to get back to herself. She had to get back to God.

24

"It's sale time, Lisa, and you've got some hard decisions to make." AC pressed. Surely he had seen how weary and drained Lisa looked, but he spoke as if he felt compelled to make her see the situation she had put the family in and deal with it.

"What's that supposed to mean?" she shot back. Even in her sorrow, she was a fighter. Who did he think he was, sitting across from her in the booth at Denny's, hiding behind his huge mustache and cool eyes, and telling her what she needed to do?

"In ranching, there is sale time, when you have to get rid of the culls. You might have a heifer that shows good potential and has good definition and a good disposition, but if she's been open for a year or two, you just have to cull her, even though you hate to. It is just the way it is to get to the bottom line of productivity."

"And your point is?"

He shrugged his shoulders, "Sometimes life is like ranching."

"Stop judging me," She said flatly.

"I'm not judging you."

"Yes you are, I can see it in your eyes. I already know I'm guilty."

"Well, I'm thrilled you are looking at my eyes."

"And what is that supposed to mean?" she shot back.

"I had a little boy call me today, trying to get me to see and pay attention. He tried to act nonchalant, but that boy was scared spitless. I think he's been trying to get someone to look and pay attention for awhile now."

Lisa stared into the coffee cup in her hands. She clicked her metallic reddish-copper painted nails absently against the ceramic cup. Her coffee was thick with cream and sweetener.

"I wasn't a very good friend, just letting you all go like that, without standing up." He spoke softly, stirring the children's hot chocolate the waitress had just placed in front of the 3 that were closest to him in the large circular booth.

"**Letting** us go?"

"Oh, come on now, Lisa, don't get all riled, I just mean that a good friend, who sees the possibility of a train wreck ahead, shouldn't just let the other friend charge along into it without at least sayin' something. I shouldn't have just watched you go, with a pain inside.

"You, the perfect Mr. Greening, know about train wrecks?" She spoke out of her own pain.

"I've had a few." There was a long pause between them. AC finally broke the silence. "Why did you move down to Phoenix?"

"I moved there for this job. To make a living for the family."

"No you didn't"

" I certainly did. I had a good job. The kids were in good schools. Matty was finally in a school that understood him, and the kids had good opportunities available to them"

AC looked into her eyes, his blue eyes piercing. There was something fierce in them. "You moved down there because that hustler worked it all out for you...because he knows you like someone to take care of you." His bluntness was astounding.

"Listen, I don't need anybody to take care of me..."

"I didn't say need," he interrupted, "I said want. That is what Grant did- he took care of you and the kids, and you miss that. You want somebody to take care of you again...you just have the wrong man for the job."

"Just leave Grant out of this, and you don't know everything about me." The walls were closing in on her. He did know her. He knew her like a book, and that thought suddenly scared her. She looked at Matthew in the large, circular booth, his hair tousled, Jacob leaning on his shoulder, and Peter huddled against him. On the other side were John and Becky, snuggled head to head. A pang of conviction started in the pit of her soul and reached out to snatch her entire being in remorse and sorrow. She needed air and space. She needed to think, and more so, to pray. What had she done with God since Grant had died? Where had He gone? Where had she gone to run away?

They spent the next 30 minutes eating and drinking, without much more than small talk with the tired children.

***

Suddenly she thought of Grant. She thought of the validity of AC's comments.

Maybe that is what Grant had been. He had been their safety valve, saving her and her family from her own incredible selfishness and pride, reminding her that her family was infinitely more important than her career or reputation, or station in life. How had she lost track of that? How had she gotten to this place, and where would she go from here? Brent had been her rock from the beginning. Now he was the reason for her two sullen boys and the van parked in the lot of Show Low's downtown Denny's, packed with their important belongings. There had been a time when Lisa enjoyed, even thrived on responsibility and decision-making, but not now. She felt weary, confused and small. It was imperative that she get back to Alpine. She needed to return to their home, to her own furniture, and the safety of her own bedroom in the home they had made together. Oh how she missed Grant!

"Listen," AC's voice was softer, but his eyes still cool. "It is pretty late, and everybody's stressed out." He reached into his pocket and pulled out a small roll of bills. "I'll get y'all a room at the Day's Inn next door. I'll help you get the kids there." He laid a wad of bills on the table under the ticket and spoke softly in Matty and Jacob's ears, gently rousing them.

Lisa roused herself. *He's a better father to them than I am a mother.* She watched him tenderly scoop up the two younger boys and hold them close, one on each arm.

"NO, thank you... I'm going home to Alpine... now," she stated.

"It's almost 1, Lisa, it'll take an hour and a half to get to Alpine... are you sure you don't want to rest and just head out in the mornin'?" There was genuine concern in his voice, as he stood with two boys draped over his arms.

"No...I want to get home."

"I'll follow you to Alpine, then," He stated matter-of-factly.

She nodded, as she lowered her gaze to the empty Equal packets on the table. AC turned and left. Matthew and Jacob followed him like sheep. Lisa felt alone. She bent to pick Becky up from the seat of the booth. She studied the plump face; the long dark lashes of her closed eyes. When had she grown up? How had Lisa missed it? She gathered Becky, who woke momentarily, but promptly plopped her head on Lisa's shoulder again, and she followed AC and the boys out the door. AC had swiftly gotten the boys arranged in the van by the time Lisa and Becky arrived. He took Becky and sat her in the back seat, before tucking his own Carhart jacket around her and closing the door.

He nodded a brief smile at Matty, who was now awake and looking out the front passenger window, with eyes that nearly broke his heart. AC let his fingers linger on the glass before winking and nodding.

"I'll be right behind you." His gaze was softer, but still intent.

How differently those words sounded now, than so many months ago on that rainy roadside. Again she nodded. She was close enough to catch his earthy scent, to smell the familiar Tide mingled with manly sweat. Suddenly she wanted him to hold her, to pull her close and press her head to his strong chest. To comfort her, but she figured he was not offering comfort to her today.

She felt sure that only the fact that they were in a public restaurant had restrained his anger toward her here this evening. He had not minced words with her. He had been painfully blunt about her, her children, and about Brent. She knew the truth. Now her world was shattering around her, her family was crumbling, and she had no one to lean on... or blame, but herself.

She longed to have even a little bit of what Matty seemed to have with this man. She thought of rushing to his embrace, of burying her face in his flannel shirt and letting her tears mingle with his fresh sweat at the base of his neck. But that would be to admit her defeat, her failure, and the utter chaos that her soul was in at this very moment.

Lisa slipped beneath the wheel of the van. AC walked around the back of the van, giving the back hatch 2 quick firm pats as he left.

25

Lisa took her hot tea into the living room. She walked slowly to the studio area and gazed out into the clear starry night. Silently she took the picture of Grant off the wall and returned to her bedroom.

She spoke to Grant often, and although she knew she wasn't really talking to him, and he couldn't really hear her, she knew God did, and it was therapeutic. She sat beneath the covers and held the picture in front of her. Her tears flowed freely as she looked at the face smiling back at her. She touched the cheek of the man in the picture, ran her finger over the image of his dark hair, and sobbed.

"Oh, Grant," she choked, when she could speak, "I miss you so much," her voice trailed off. "It is so hard... life is so hard without you with me.... Brent, well, Brent was with me for a while, I told you that, but I made a total disaster out of the whole situation. Oh, I don't know what I was thinking-- why I let him into my life, why I thought he would be good for our family. First he wanted to send the older boys away... and I almost did..." she whispered, "I almost did." A new wave of tears and anguish rolled over her. After a long moment, she regained composure enough to continue in a low, desperate moan, "He spent so much time with us I didn't realize the problem with the kids ... and I had to get a restraining order... and it is just a terrible mess... and I think I've lost the older boys, and everyone who has ever really cared and loved us. Oh, Grant," she sobbed aloud as she clung to the picture, "Why did you leave me??"

26

"Are you ready to go, Mom?" Lisa glanced in the mirror to see Jacob flop on the bed behind her. "In a minute," she continued to curl her hair. She was the only one not yet ready. Lisa could not help being amazed over the past several months. It had been a long hard road, but they had made it together. Rita had stuck with her and forgiven her enough to convince her into counseling for the family. Only Rita could get away with confronting Lisa's pride while still being a friend. There had been legal issues with Brent, but they had weathered that, too.

The summer had passed without incident, even though Matty had spent every possible moment at the Ranch. Jacob had tagged along often.

She had kept to herself, however, convinced that the only way to cope with life was to stay close to God and have Him as her only friend. She spent time with her children, and only when an event of theirs came up did she dare to socialize with anyone other than Rita and her husband.

Now they had been invited to the Circle A Ranch for a Labor Day Picnic. Lisa could not refuse an invitation from the man who had meant so much to the lives of her children. She had volunteered to bring two pies, which she had finished last night. She now put the final touches on her recently highlighted, brown pile of hair. Lisa was not sure why she had taken so much pain to put it up just so, but contributed it to her general feeling that things were going well. They seemed like a family again, however fragile they might all still be.

The six Taffs climbed eagerly into the mini-van and headed to the Blue. Why did she feel such a sense of excitement and anticipation? Maybe it was just the nervousness of the new recipe grasshopper pies that were in the back of the van. Whatever it was, she hoped the noisy beating of her heart would calm soon.

27

They sat in the evening cool of the spacious living room. The picnic had been at the school on the Blue, and they had returned to AC's log home an hour earlier. Hobbie and Jacob were engaged in a game of checkers in the kitchen, and they had a rapt audience. Pete was coloring on the living room floor.

"That was such a great picnic." Lisa sighed contentedly.

"Yea, folks around here sure outdo themselves for big deals like today," a big smile spread over AC's face.

"Mmm," Lisa found herself not able to resist AC's engaging grin. She quickly sobered, casting a glance toward the windows and the growing shadows. "I think we'll need to head back pretty soon. It will be dark in an hour or so."

AC jumped to his feet, a stricken look on his face. He had been enjoying the day so much that he had let it slip by without talking to her alone. He walked nervously through the house, retrieving a light jacket for each of them. "How about a little ride?" he asked, handing her the jacket. She looked at him, a little confused. "On the horses," he chuckled.

"What about the kids?" Lisa questioned.

"They appear to be duly entertained," he helped Lisa on with the jacket and led her outside, mumbling something to Hobbie on the way out.

"You can't leave just yet, Emma is in the water closet with Becky, fixin' her hair with beads and yarn," he smiled as they crunched over a small patch of gravel to the barn. "She and Hobbie never did have kids of their own, but that Emma sure does enjoy fussin' over yours." AC saddled Blaze and a gentle mare, and held out a hand to help Lisa mount.

"I'm not sure about this, AC, I don't know how to ride."

He lifted her onto the mare's back and helped her settle into the saddle. He handed her the reins and winked. "Don't worry... all you have to do is hold on...she'll follow ol' Blaze here." He rubbed the horse's neck and patted it softly.

"You seem to have taken a little down turn after dinner," he observed.

"Hmm... just grieving a little, I suppose"

"Oh."

"Not just about Grant, but about all the mistakes I've made with my kids." Being with AC always made her mistakes glare in her mind.

"Well, I guess that's the part about God that I like the best... forgiveness. It doesn't matter how much I foul up. I can just run to Him and visit with Him about it... and He forgives."

She shook her head and looked at him, "You have such a pure and simple faith."

"Well, I reckon that goes with a simple mind."

The twinkle in his eye was not wasted on her, and she thought she saw the right corner of his mustache raise. All her guilt faded away. She returned his smile, "You are an amazing man."

"Ha!" He laughed out loud. "I have been called lots of things in my life, but amazing hasn't ever been one of 'em!"

AC led the mare for what seemed like eternity, both forms huddled against the growing chill, neither speaking. The cowboy searched his mind for something to say. Something that would touch her, move her, endear her to him. Something that would help her to know who he was and why he wanted her.

"This is the way to look at the grass, you know... you get right out in it," AC spoke knowledgeably. *Well, that sure was a romantic thought, ol' boy.*

AC reined up and pointed to the west at the shimmering horizon. They both sat on the mounts, breathless at the awesome beauty of the scene before them. AC dismounted and let the reins drop over the saddle horn. He lifted Lisa down beside him. He took his time removing his hands from her waist, holding her close for several long seconds.

His tender eyes were still looking at hers when he spoke, "Well, this is it, the Circle A Ranch. We can see most of it from here." He turned again to the west. "As far as you can see in that direction is the boundary on that side," he motioned with his hand. Then he swept to the right, "And the fence line way up there is the Northern boundary." A huge grin lighted his face as he looked at her again before turning toward the east. "You see that ridge in the distance, past the tops of those trees?"

"Uh huh," Lisa nodded, although she didn't even know what a ridge was, and she was not entirely sure which trees he was referring to.

"Well, over that ridge is the eastern border. Then to the south of the house and Jimmy Joe's place, on the other side of the road is a little bit, maybe a few hundred acres, but this is basically it." He moved his arm slowly in an arc before him and beamed. "There's three houses, and then of course the barns and out buildings and such." He searched her eyes for some type of reaction besides bewilderment. Seeing none, he launched into a
speech that he had been working on for a long time, hoping that he would get through it, and that she would finally know his feelings for her.

"Well, I just wanted to thank you for sharing your son, and, shoot...all of your kids with me." He looked down at the dirt and tried not to shuffle his feet. "And I'm mighty thankful to God for giving me this place and all, and well, I was thinking that I could share a bit with... you know..." he stopped suddenly, and grabbed her hand, looking directly into her blue-green eyes, almost burning a hole through her, but surely warming her to the core. " I believe I'm in love with you, Lisa," he started earnestly, "and your kids are just great, and...well...I know I'm not what you had, but I'd surely like to share all this with you...and the kids...if you give us- you and me together- a chance, I don't think you would be disappointed." His eyes pleaded with her as he pressed on, "You don't have to say anything right now, but you can just take a little bit to think on it and let it roll around in your mind for a while, but I would like you to ponder it considerably." He was trying to use words that he wouldn't normally use, and purposefully concentrated on making sure all the words that needed it had the *ing* ending fully on them, so she would not

104

be swayed by the thought that he was merely a simple-minded, hick-speaking cowboy.

Just then he realized that he hadn't removed his hat before talking to her. He knew he should have snatched it off of his head right then, but her hand felt so warm and good, enveloped in both of his, that he was not willing to let it go. Not even one hand.

Lisa reached her other hand to rest on AC's hands. She blushed profusely, "You have a great place here, AC, and you have made such a big impact on Matthew in particular. Working with you and the animals has been so wonderful for Matty, it has made all the difference for him, it is just what he has needed." Now it was her turn to look at the ground. She could not risk losing herself in his big blue eyes. " My heart is just in such a jumble, AC."

He lifted her chin with one warm hand and saw the tears. Blinking furiously to keep back his own fears that she would reject him, he pulled her close and tangled his hand in her dark nutty hair. He relished the scent of her and finally whispered, "Think
about it...would you do that, Lisa... just think about it for a while? I sure would like for you to be in the "circle" of the Circle A Ranch." He knew it sounded corny, but it was all he had.

Lisa straightened. Resolve was evident in her face. "I'm so sorry, AC, I don't want to be ungrateful or anything, and I hope your relationship with Matthew is not contingent on us being anything else but good friends… and you have been a good friend, but I just spent the last several months getting my life and family back together, just really finding myself and trying to get myself together. You were the one who said to me that I don't need a man to hang my arm on. I don't think I can love anyone else, or get married again. Not just to you, but to anyone."

Her words hit him like a kick of a calf's leg. He kept his voice and composure even. "How about just thinking about it for a while. I don't want to press you, and I know we got started kind of rocky, but please say you will think about it." He held her gaze.

Amazingly, she looked sadly back into his eyes. "I can't think about it any more, AC. I'm out for the good of my children, and only that. You are a wonderful man, and a true friend - second only to Rita," she chuckled, "But I can't be anything more. I can't marry you, AC... I'm sorry."

28

Lisa looked again at the picture smiling at her in the moonlight. She pushed back the covers and reached to grasp it close to her. Fresh tears welled in her already red eyes. It had been a long ride home from the Circle A Ranch.

"Oh, Grant," she choked, "There is a man who has been taking good care of Matty, uh... that's Matthew, and he seems to adore all of the children. He has been so helpful. He has been working with Matty, and Matty is really growing and seems to be doing so much better. He has this huge mustache," Lisa smiled in spite of herself, "And he actually shaved it off for awhile, because Becky didn't like it! Can you imaging that?" Lisa chuckled. Then she caught herself and quickly sobered. "Well, he is a very sweet and kind man, and the children have really taken to him. He is so good, and the kids love him, and I know I already said that, but,... he... he said that he thinks he loves me...thinks he loves us... and I ... I think... well, I mean, I ... oh, I don't know what I think...or feel. Oh Arlow, why do you have to crowd into every private conversation I try to have?" She clutched the picture to her chest, as fresh tears coursed her cheeks. "I told him no, Grant. I told him no. I had to tell him no."

When Lisa awoke, the clock read 3:00 am. She felt exhausted, still, and put Grant's picture on her nightstand. Without thinking too much about it, she shuffled down the hall to check on the kids, before remembering to turn out the kitchen light, and made her way back to the lonely bedroom. When sleep finally found her, it was nearly time to start another day.

Lisa moved through the next few days as if on autopilot. She altered between feeling too much and blocking all feeling from her. She thought her answer to Arlow would end her confusion, but it seemed to bring on a new wave. She prayed, as she had never prayed before, and the answer appeared to be clear. When she looked at her children however, all she could see was the mustached rancher's brand of love upon them.

29

There was still a slight strain between them as AC sat in Lisa's living room. Labor Day was two months past, and life moved on. AC had dropped Jacob and Matty off and Lisa had invited him to sit for a cup of coffee. He had felt uncomfortable trying to be "good friends" with Matty's mother, but he recalled Clay's influence on his own life and tried to keep on friendly terms for the boy's sake.

"You doin' OK?" he asked as he sipped the steaming black liquid.

"Yes, " she paused slightly, "I think we're doing very well right now." She smiled that knock out smile that usually got to him.

"That's great," he said evenly. Maybe he was over her. "You seem pretty content, and the boys seem to be doin' fine in school. They always do good at the ranch, and I sure appreciate you lettin' 'em come down."

"There may be an opening at the Blue School next year," AC finally spoke again over the top of his coffee mug, "I'm confident that if you'd like the job, it's yours."

Lisa raised a questioning eyebrow.

The right side of his mustache rose slightly, and his eyes softened momentarily. "Seein' as Hobbie is on the school board."

"What's happening to the current teacher? Miss Hinkle, isn't it? The boys have mentioned her a time or two lately. Did we meet her at the Labor Day picnic?"

AC winced internally at the thought of the picnic "Yea...yea, you did. I think Miss Hinkle will be getting married after the first of the year. She'll be helping her husband on the ranch." AC's deep blue eyes remained fixed on hers, hoping she could not read them. "She'll still be in the area...she'll still be on the Blue... but just not teachin'. I'm sure she'd be all the help you'd need with any questions."

"I don't have a teaching certificate. I've never taught children...except for once when I was an assistant in Sunday School," she rolled her eyes at the mere remembrance of that fiasco.

"Things like that aren't even an itty-bitty problem," he assured her. "Teachers for the Blue aren't exactly easy to come by, and Hobbie is talking all the time about the State being willing to work with the school. Miss Hinkle came on some kind of a special deal that let her take classes and teach at the same time. I believe that it took her a year or two to become all legal. I'm just stating a possibility. You can talk to Hobbie if you take a mind to. The college here has extension courses in Springerville, and even some correspondence. Just thought I'd mention it."

"Thanks, AC, I appreciate you telling me. I may look into it." Her voice was warm and sweet, but her eyes held concern in them.

30

Emma bustled around the kitchen of the ranch headquarters like a young girl. "I am surely glad you've come out of that little tailspin you were in," Emma patted AC's shoulder as she poured hot coffee into his mug.

"Now, Emma, don't be actin' like a psychiatrist," Hobbie shot his wife a glance between bites of green beans.

"And I'm glad Melissa Hinkle is coming over again tonight," She ignored Hobbie's gaze.

"Oh Emma, you've been trying to match ol' AC here up with Missy Hinkle for a long time," Hobbie huffed.

"And now I can quit," she proclaimed. Hobbie nudged her hip with his elbow as she turned away. "I think it's mighty nice of you showing her the ropes of the ranch. And she will be here for Thanksgiving. I will show her how to roast the turkey just so. I can give her my recipe book!" The thought brightened Emma's face.

"Hmmph." AC looked at Emma and Hobbie before returning to his mashed potatoes.

"She asked me to help her with the wedding dress, you know," Emma continued, undaunted, as she took her place at the table.

"You are carryin' on like it is your wedding," Hobbie groused.

"There is nothing wrong with being excited. It isn't every day that folks on the Blue get married. It couldn't happen to a nicer couple, " Emma glanced at AC.

"Well, she don't have no ring on her finger yet," Hobbie stated.

"She will," AC rose as he saw Melissa Hinkle's truck come up the drive. He mashed his cowboy hat on his head as he walked toward the door.

31

"Mom, its for you," Jacob handed Lisa the phone that she had not heard ring. A pile of bills was arrayed in front of her as she sat at the kitchen table. A huge smile graced Jacob's face as he met his mother's tired eyes and then dashed outside to join his siblings at play.

"Hello," Lisa's voice had an edge to it.

"Hello...Lisa?" AC's voice was low and warm, and sent a sweet tingle down Lisa's back. "Everythin' goin' along alright?"

"Oh, hello, Arlow...yes, we're fine, thank you," she replied, although she felt anything but fine.

AC did not recalled when Lisa had started calling him by his given name, but she had. Not that she used the name in anyone else's presence, no, she had promised him that. Only when she spoke directly to him, with no one else in hearing range, did she use the name that had until now been reserved only for his mother. Although it sent a flush of embarrassment up his face each time he heard it, he was not about to tell the young lady with painted nails and dangling earrings not to call him that.

"Well then, I was calling because I need to work out some details on the family ranch up yond..." he corrected himself, "...uh, up in Wyoming, and I need to jump on up there for a week or two, or maybe even through Christmas. It has come up sudden like, and I wanted to talk with you and Matty about it and change the schedule for him coming to the ranch a little bit. Maybe Matty and whoever else wants to could spend part of the school break after Christmas down here." AC knew that his proposition was bold. He also knew that he had stated his trip as truthfully as he could. He had to make a change in his personal life, and desperately needed the wise counsel of his family.

He was sure that once he arrived home, the first visit in the past two years, he would not want to leave the company of his siblings and the myriad of nieces and nephews. Lisa had said nothing about her plans for Christmas, and AC did not feel like spending this Christmas at the ranch, so near to Lisa, and yet so far.

"Oh...sure..." she choked. She had no idea why tears suddenly welled in her eyes, but she chalked it up to hormones and stress, as she pressed on, "Matty will be disappointed, but it is so busy for them in school right now, and things going on at the church, it is probably good that he won't be running to your place for a couple of weeks." Her voice was shaky but she simply said, "Hold on and I'll get Matty"

Matty ran in to answer the phone. Whatever AC said, and however he said it, Matty took it well, much better than Lisa had. He did not seem to be upset at all. He chattered on for several minutes and finally returned the receiver to his mother, a sheepish grin on his face.

"Well, whatever you said, it sure was the right thing." Lisa was amazed at the way AC handled her oldest son. She composed considerably.

"I guess you could say we came to an agreement on the matter that suited both of us." AC replied. Lisa could hear the smile in AC's voice, and somehow, it made her want to cry again.

Lisa suddenly realized a yearning to meet AC's family. She wanted to know where he came from and details about him. She thought of strolling into the presence of his large family on Arlow's arm. A gasp escaped her lips, partly for the thought, and partly to stifle a rising sob. She had had the chance to be close to him, and she had rejected it. He had made his feelings known, and she had rejected them. He had moved on, and until this moment, she had, too.

"Are you sure you are gettin' along alright, darlin'?"

A long silence halted any further conversation. AC had used a term of endearment, and it seemed that neither knew quite what to say. Moments passed in awkward silence.

"Lisa?"

"Yes...yes, I'll be fine," she whispered. "Listen, the kids are getting into it...I have to check on them...have a good trip..."

"Lisa?" AC interrupted.

"Yes?"

"I'll call to check on you all when I get back, OK?"

"OK."

" See ya," he blurted out hastily, before hanging up.

32

There was a shriek as the front porch door swung open, and Rosalinda, AC's half sister, bounded out and down the steps to greet the incoming truck. AC had barely stepped out of the cab of his brother's truck when she threw her arms around his neck, nearly knocking him off balance. He managed to reach up just in time to keep his hat from toppling off.

"How you been, Rosy?" AC mumbled into her rich chestnut hair. She stepped back and flashed her wide smile before burying herself again in his powerful embrace.

AC glanced over her at Evelyn, his mother, hanging back on the porch steps. She wasn't beyond running out to greet her youngest boy herself, but today she stood as though she would let AC climb the steps to her. After all, he had taken long enough to come back home.

Rosy released AC's neck and followed him as he quickly made his way to his mother's outstretched arms. Her warm body seemed small in his arms, and her familiar scent warmed his heart.

"Mama!" he whispered into her ear as he kissed her cheek and gently lifted her off the ground. He held her firmly in the strength of his lonesome arms several moments before setting her feet back on the porch. Evelyn held AC at arm's length, tears
glistening on her cheeks.

It took only a minute for mama to compose herself. "I see Everett's brought my long lost boy back," she looked deep

116

into his eyes, her own blue eyes overflowing with love and affirmation.

"Its so good to see you, mama," AC replied, wiping the sun's glare out of his eyes with the back of his hand. Soon the porch and yard was bustling with brothers, sisters, nieces and nephews, all clamoring for hugs, kisses, and the latest news from the only sibling of the family who did not live within a 150 mile radius of mama's house.

The evening had passed in a joyous hubbub of sharing news, devouring favorite family dishes and meeting the latest additions to the family, 18-month-old twins. It was good to be home, in the center of the family activity and love he so cherished.

He remembered being chided by them all for not going to college for the very reason that he simply could not bring himself to leave the ranch. Not even for the time it would take to finish just one semester of university work. He loved the land too much. He loved caring for the livestock entrusted to him on the ranch, and every detail of ranch life. Not only did he love it, he knew it well and was good at the business of a cow-calf operation. Besides, he had seen what university had done to his older siblings. They had all left the ranch. Janie had married a soil conservation specialist, which was all right in and of itself, but he had moved her to Cheyenne for some university job.

Everett and Wes had both become teachers and had taken jobs at the local school. The twins, Lewis and Louise had both married, and while they were still nearby, they were definitely not involved in the home ranch, except for gathering, branding and shipping, when everyone pitched in to help mama. Russ and his wife raised horses on a ranch nearby. Donald, the brother just older than AC had been to college and had come back with a head full of new ideas. Many of them were good ideas, but AC thought that Donald tended to look down his nose at Clay since he had returned from school.

AC could learn just fine, had learned just fine up to that point, from Clay and Mama, and the ranch itself. Clay had always said that the cattle and the land would give a person clues as to how to take better care of the ranch.

Dustie had graduated from college, and she and Rosalinda were the ones who still ranched along with mama, and generally took care of the place, along with Roy, the hired hand that Clay had inherited from AC's daddy. He had been with daddy, and the Ranch as long as AC could remember, and AC thought Roy was old way back then. The truth was, the only thing in the world that Roy knew was cowboying, and he was content to cowboy on the C Bar Ranch for a small stipend and a place to room and ride. Dustie was a leading barrel racer in the state. She and her husband of two years seemed to be having the time of their lives, living in the old bunkhouse, working the ranch and rodeoing. Rosalinda had started college, but decided that working at the local insurance office, and working the ranch on the weekends was a better fit for her.

"I expect you'll ride with me in the mornin'," mama said before kissing her youngest son goodnight.

"I sure will, mama," AC had said, "You still rise at 5:30?"

"Breakfast will be on the table by that time," mama winked and blew AC another kiss before retreating behind her bedroom door.

AC was left in the stillness of the large kitchen, which only hours before had been abuzz with activity. Every sibling had gathered at mama's house to enjoy the precious time together. There were children running and riding everywhere. Dustie and Lewis had set up a roping, and young and old had tried their hand at snagging the elusive roping dummy in the wide alley of the huge barn just behind the hill that mama's house was on. The older generation had displayed how it was done, when the games turned to tabletop roping later in the afternoon in the family room of the house. The activity of family thrilled his heart, and he looked forward to tomorrow, when gatherings were again planned.

AC found his way to the room that used to be his. It was basically the same as he had last left it, and it comforted him some. His mama's words rang in his ears. Of course he would ride with her in the morning. Did she need to ask? Ever since he was old enough to dress himself he had gotten up in the pre-dawn each morning and ridden with one of his brothers or Clay himself, to check the fence line and waters. Clay was very particular about his drinkers, about everything, actually.

Clay viewed ranching much like a preacher would view a ministry. To Clay, ranching was a ministry. He lived by the scripture that said that whatever you do, do it all as unto the Lord. Everything Clay did on the ranch and with mama and his brother's children was done as to the Lord Himself. He tended each cow, each horse, and each pasture as to the Lord. He had taken the task of tending to his brother's wife and children as to the Lord also. Oh, Everett and the older boys had balked at his authority and ways at the beginning, but AC knew that when Everett had needed a daddy the most, in his teenage years, Clay had been there for him. Everett had confided that to AC after Clay had passed on six years ago.

Somewhere in the midst of realizing how much he missed Clay, remembering how good it was to be home, looking forward to riding with mama in the morning, and missing Matty, AC passed into the REM sleep he needed so much.

The smell of bacon and coffee brought AC to his feet before the light of day. The air was crisp and cold, but he heard a fire crackling in the wood stove in the big room. AC washed and slipped into suitable riding clothes and headed to the kitchen. He had overslept, intending to have built the fire for the day, and have the horses saddled and ready to go by now. He walked to the stove where mama stood before a pan of frying potatoes. He hugged her from behind and placed a loving kiss on her right cheek. She lifted a hand to his cheek, reveling in her son's presence.

"I'm sorry I'm up late, mama," he whispered, lingering in his hug and at her cheek, "I'll go saddle the horses."

She pressed his cheek against hers. "Why don't you wait until we've had a good breakfast? I'm not so feeble yet that I can't saddle my own horse," she teased.

They walked down the slight incline to the barn together. It was a huge enclosure, with ten stalls on one side, and another two on the other side. Next to the ten stalls was a spacious tack room with saddletrees neatly placed around the room, a rail covered with saddle blankets along the left wall, and tack hung orderly on the far wall. To the right were shelves that held grooming tools and vet supplies. The far three-quarters of the barn was open space, which was stacked to the tin roof with hay. It opened into the pasture that the cattle wintered in. The near one- quarter of the barn held a large room filled with bags of feed and other sundry supplies. Between the two sides of stalls was enough space for three pickups to drive side by side.

As they entered the barn, AC could almost smell the scent of Clay. It was peppermint, mingled with Old Spice, but he knew his mind was just playing tricks with him. They saddled the horses together in the chill of the morning, and rode into the winter pasture. They followed a row of feeders, which gave way to a long line of widely placed, mostly eaten, bales of hay. Although December was usually a snowy month at the ranch, this year the snow had not arrived. The ground was hard beneath their feet, but there was no snow on the ground…yet.

They had checked the fence line of the nearest pasture and checked on all the waters by the time they turned their horses for home. It had been a long morning, and AC was grateful for such a long visit alone with mama. Not that they had talked the whole time. No, he and mama could enjoy each other's company just fine without having to say a word.

He had done most of the talking this morning. He had a ring in his pocket; he just wasn't sure what to do with it. It was mama who spoke now. Mama, whose heart had felt it all, whose eyes had seen both sadness and joy through all the tears she had cried, whose spirit and resolve and strength of character outshone that of any woman he had ever known.

"You know, Arlow, the Lord told me after your daddy died that Clay would take care of me. He just spoke to me and said, *Clay will take care of you.* Those were His very words. I didn't know how that would be, but I had to trust the Lord. I didn't have any idea that Clay would actually marry me to do that. You know he was a few years younger than I." She glanced at AC, a slight smile gracing her lips. AC continued riding slowly in silence, waiting for her to continue.

"I never thought he would marry me and take on all of you children, but he did... even though..." she hesitated, "even though he...well, let's just say that love grows, Arlow, love grows if you are patient and let it, and heart lines are stronger than bloodlines
sometimes."

"I don't know, Mama, this woman is just like a burr under my blanket sometimes."

"You know about loving... and losing... and loving again." She had stopped her horse, as he had, and was looking into his blue eyes with her own. "You know," she repeated. And he did. He knew. He reached his hand to take hers, squeezed it and lifted it to his lips. He brushed her fingers with the tickle of his mustache. He sat back and looked at his mama, huddled in her Carhart jacket sitting there strong in her saddle. Her eyes were soft and knowing.

"Sometimes it is trouble that spurs you on to higher things."

33

AC had returned early with a fresh confidence and resolve about him, the diamond studded garnet ring still in his pocket. He was indeed encouraged and advised by everyone in his family.

It was 4:00 pm when AC picked up the phone and heard Matty's frightened voice.

"AC, AC, everybody's sick here... the kids are being sick in the bathroom, and my mom's sick too... she's moaning on the bed... and I don't think that she can get up." The panic rose in Matty's voice as he continued, "Mom told me this morning to get ahold of the pastor or Rita, but neither one of them is home!"

After several questions and some quick instructions, AC and Doc Hayden, a MD from Tucson who had the ranch next to the Circle A, headed for Alpine.

AC's sister Dustie and her husband Tom, who was a beginning pilot and had flown them all back to Arizona from Wyoming several days earlier, went to work fixing beds and gathering supplies for taking care of a family with the flu. Melissa Hinkle helped with the preparations.

Once in Alpine, Doc Hayden examined the family and traded vehicles with AC. Hayden took the 4 wheel drive Silverado quad cab to town for additional medical supplies, and AC took Hayden's Suburban loaded with toiletries, clothes, blankets and sick bodies back to the Blue with him. Emma and Dustie immediately took charge of the three little children, while Jacob and Matty helped AC and Melissa get Lisa settled into the master bedroom.

***

Lisa vaguely remembered being lifted from her bed and bounced along, and now she was being carried and set down again. She tried to speak, to move, but her limbs would not respond to her feeble commands, and her words came out as moans. Heat enveloped her as she entered the dessert of sickness. Her whole body, and especially her head ached. Her body convulsed on its own, heaving involuntarily as waves of nausea overtook and consumed her. Fever overwhelmed her and held her down in clouds of darkness.

For the next several days, she floated in and out of awareness. There was always a strong arm tending her. Soothing her. Helping her whenever the elevator of consciousness brought her to ground level. His soft words rested in her ears. His scent lingered in her mind, long after the heat of her fever pushed her down into the darkness where she lay beyond his reach. Still, she knew he was there.

"It's OK, Lisa. I'm here with you. You're going to be OK." AC whispered as he dabbed her forehead and face with a tepid wet cloth.

"Oh Grant," Lisa moaned feverishly

"*Grant? Grant!*" AC knew she was delirious with the fever, and yet the word hit him like a stallion's hooves. He wondered if she would ever be able to love anyone else. He sat somberly in the bedside chair and wondered if it was his daddy that his own mama saw when she had looked into Clay's eyes. The thought was too much for him to dwell on.

AC walked out to the kitchen, leaving a cool washcloth on Lisa's forehead. Emma had three small glasses of lemon-lime soda on a tray in the kitchen, and the wash machine going in the mudroom. She looked at AC through tired eyes. AC managed a smile beneath his mustache.

"You'd best go lie down and take a snooze, Miss Emma, you look all done in," AC headed for the serving tray.

"You look about the same," the plump woman chortled.

"Yea, but since I'm not as beautiful as you, I don't need as much beauty rest," He winked and motioned with his head for her to go to her room.

He grabbed the tray and headed up the stairs to where the three smallest of Lisa's children were recovering from the flu. Becky looked much better. She was sitting up in the bed with her doll in front of her. She smiled at AC and dutifully drank sips of the soda until it was gone. Peter and John were not faring so well, although Peter was better than John. AC did manage to get both boys to drink some of the soda before leaving them each with a fresh cool washcloth on their foreheads.

By evening, Becky was dressed and walking around the house. Hobbie walked over to the bunkhouse, where those without the bug were staying with AC's sister Dustie and her husband Tom, and Melissa Hinkle.

AC continued to keep a vigil with Lisa. After a long nap, Emma was again up and tending to the little boys. Hobbie had taken on the job of chores around the ranch with the willing and able help of Tom, Matty and Jacob.

On the afternoon of Christmas Eve, Dustie had insisted on getting a Christmas tree up in the living room of the ranch headquarters. She and Tom enlisted the help of Lisa's children. All except John joined in the festivities eagerly. He was content to sit quietly on one of the couches and doze while he "supervised." Tom and Hobbie delighted everyone by playing Christmas carols and other tunes on the harmonica and fiddle. Everyone sucked leisurely on peppermint sticks, the only sweet that Emma would allow anyone, for fear of starting the whole plague over again.

Lisa still lay hot beneath the light covers in AC's room. AC appeared long enough in the living room to offer prayers of thanks for the children's recovery and earnest pleas for Lisa's recovery as well. With exhausted eyes and body, he hugged everyone goodnight and returned to the room where Lisa lay.

Hours later, Dustie entered the room; silently pulling a chair next to the one AC was sitting in. She could see the worry in his eyes as he rested his elbows on his knees and cradled his chin in his palms. She set a delicate, yet calloused hand on his strong shoulder.

"She's goin' to be OK." she whispered in his ear, "All of you are going to be just fine." Dustie hoped that she had sounded positive as she glanced pensively at the form in the bed. This fever had lasted too long.

34

Lisa heard distant voices as she rose to consciousness. Her eyes fluttered open and she looked at the dark ceiling. Where was she? She scanned the room, feeling dizzy with even the slightest movement of her head. A dim light filtered out from behind a half closed door on the far side of the room. Several feet to her left sat two huddled figures. She was sweating profusely, and knew that she needed help in getting to the bathroom. She tried to speak, but only managed a small moan and a grunt.

Instantly, a young man was at her side. *AC!* She smiled faintly. "I... have... to..." she barely whispered. AC jumped up, grabbed a large mixing bowl from the floor beside the bed, gently raised Lisa's head, pillow and all, to an almost sitting position, and held the bowl in front of her. He waited, as if expecting something to happen.

"No...I..." Lisa croaked out.

"Oh...OK," AC nodded, as he slowly laid her head back on the bed and returned the bowl to the floor. A tall woman appeared at AC's side, and they took Lisa between them.

"She's wringin' wet," Dustie commented as they half carried, half walked Lisa through the door into the dim light of the bathroom. AC instantly disappeared. It was then that Lisa noticed she was wearing a large flannel shirt for a nightgown. She sat on the commode and the slender woman turned on the water in the sink. An arm thrust through the door holding out a clean flannel shirt and Lisa's robe. They acted with a precision pattern that indicated that they might have done this same thing several times before. Lisa's head swam with minimal exertion on her part.

"AC!" Dustie called as she draped Lisa in the fresh shirt and held her shoulders, "She's gonna faint on us!"

AC appeared and lifted her slowly and gingerly in his strong arms. Dustie clutched the front of the shirt closed and threw Lisa's robe over the top of her. AC carried Lisa back to the bed, which sported a clean fresh bottom sheet. The covers were still in a heap on the floor and the clean top sheet was draped at the foot of the bed.

AC laid Lisa tenderly on the bed. "Go on, you," Dustie said and motioned AC away with her head. "I'll fix her up." AC turned and smiled at Dustie, brushing his mustache across her forehead. Dustie's hands deftly buttoned the flannel shirt around Lisa, slipped the robe off of her and the fresh covers back up over her waist. She turned to let AC take over, after sending a sweet smile to Lisa's eyes. AC sat on the bed next to Lisa and put a hand on each of her shoulders.

"Howdy," he smiled. It was the cleverest thing he could think of in the middle of this night. He touched her forehead and cheeks with his large calloused hands. Lisa managed another weak smile.

Dustie gathered the laundry from the bathroom and bedroom floor and headed for the door. "See you in the morning," she called.

"Thanks, Dustie," AC's clear voice rang through the room as Dustie exited.

AC turned back to Lisa. Her eyes were still open and confused.

"Are you thirsty?" he asked softly.

Lisa nodded. He held the cool glass to her lips and she drank greedily. She would have gulped the entire glass full had he let her. "Whoa, girl," he chuckled as he slipped the glass away from her lips and replaced her head on the pillow. "We want that to stay with you for awhile." She managed another weak smile, although she longed to grab the water and gulp it down. AC seemed to read her mind and her confused eyes. "I'll give you some more in a minute," he smiled and looked into her sea-green eyes. He spoke to explain; "I came back from Wyoming about a week ago. I left a message on your machine. Then Matty called me and asked me to come and help him. He said everyone was sick, including you, and he didn't know what to do. We came up and picked you all up a few days ago and brought you all here," he smiled sheepishly. "You were pretty much out of it with the fever and the bug the past several days.

"We?" Lisa quizzed shakily.

"Me, Melissa Hinkle and my neighbor, Doc Hayden" AC looked suddenly uneasy. " Doc looked in on everyone. He gave you 3 shots in all, and said not to let you dehydrate. He's been checking on y'all every day." AC kept looking into her eyes, he seemed glad to see them open again. "The kids are all better... we've just been waiting on you, now." Even beneath his mustache, she could tell he was smiling, but she gave way to the heaviness in her eyelids without saying anything more.

35

When Lisa awoke again, AC was slumped over in a chair beside her bed, his head resting at her left thigh, just at her fingertips. She let her fingers rest in his tousled golden hair. His head jerked up and he grunted awake. A smile brightened his eyes as he saw she was awake.

"How ya feelin'?" his voice was still laced with sleep.

"Better." Lisa put on her biggest smile for this cowboy who was nursing her back to herself.

He touched her shoulder. "I sure am glad this fever is leavin' you, but you're soaked again," he frowned, feeling the dampness of his flannel shirt she was wearing. He said hoarsely, "I'll get Dustie or Missy to help you."

With all of her available strength, she grabbed his arm as he rose to go. "Arlow..." she made an effort to flash him a smile.

"Yes, ma'am?" he seemed to answer naturally without thinking.

"Thank you," she whispered through misty eyes.

He cleared his throat and brought her hand to his mustache. "You're welcome."

Dustie entered the bedroom several minutes later carrying Lisa's silk peach pajamas over her arm. Matty had packed them for her before they hastily left their house, days earlier.

"Good mornin', honey," she said cheerily. Her tone was sisterly and in no way condescending. "You feelin' a little better?" Her eyes danced in the morning sun gushing through the windows.

Lisa nodded and smiled. She liked this woman.

"We'd better get you changed again, and don't worry about that, 'cause when you come from a big family like mine, you don't pay too much attention to people dressin' and undressin' with each other around," Dustie said as she bustled around the room. She offered Lisa a glass of the lemon-lime soda that Emma had sent in with her, "I get to help you get up and around this mornin', if you care to." Dustie lifted Lisa's head and shoulders and helped her sit up in the bed. The thought of having a stranger see her like this and how she must have been the past few days did unnerve her a little. Somehow this young perky woman made Lisa feel like she had known her forever, and this sudden intimacy just a part of that long friendship.

"Do you feel up to a bath?" Dustie quizzed. "I'll help you in there, and if you get too weak and dizzy, you'll already be sitting down, and you can just lean back and close your eyes." She looked eagerly at Lisa.

"Yes," Lisa said, "I'd like to try, anyway."

"Good."

Dustie continued to chatter merrily as she helped Lisa slowly to the bathroom, sat her on the closed seat of the commode, and poured some shampoo into the running bath water to create some soothing bubbles.

"I bet AC didn't even tell you that I'm his baby sister, huh?"

Lisa shook her head at the slender woman in the tight jeans and denim shirt. Her sandy hair was in a French braid tied with a red ribbon. Lisa knew exactly which nail polish on her bedroom bureau would look great with the outfit. The young woman wore no make-up. She didn't need any.

"Those kids of yours are sure sweethearts. Little Becky and I hit it off right away. Shucks, I'd take her home with me if she wasn't so attached to her mamma." Dustie flashed a bright smile that revealed straight white teeth. "She said she had to stay here and take care of you." She swished the water to stir up additional bubbles. "Tom and I don't have any kids yet...we're still at the stage of havin' fun tryin'," she giggled and shot an impish grin at Lisa. "I'll tell you who just loves your kids, though...it's Melissa."

"Melissa?" Lisa squeaked.

"Melissa Hinkle, the bride to be. She is getting a good taste of what children will be all about."

"Oh."

"The water is ready here, let me help you in and then I'll leave you in private, but I am going to leave the door open while I change that bed, in case you need to holler for me." Dustie helped Lisa out of her sweaty nightclothes and into the tub.

The water felt warm and wonderful as it rolled over Lisa's weak body. She did have to rest her head against the back of the tub several times, as she washed the sickness away.

Dustie knocked on the door after several long minutes. "You doin' alright in there? I don't want to rush you, but stayin' in the hot water for too long will take the wind outa your sails for sure."

"I'm finished," Lisa managed.

Dustie handed the towel around the shower curtain and left her hand there for Lisa to grab it as she stood up. She helped Lisa to a small stool to sit. Instantly Dustie had another towel and was using it to dry Lisa's tangled hair.

Lisa could not figure out why she was not irate at this woman's bold care of her, but Dustie didn't seem to think twice of the care she was giving to this stranger. AC could not give her this intimate level of care. Lisa needed the care, and Dustie matter-of-factly was giving it. Lisa sat there weakly, feeling like she was the little sister in it all, too tired to object to Dustie combing her hair and helping her back to the bed. She collapsed into the clean sheets and lapsed into a sleep of exhaustion instead of fever for the first time in four days.

36

Melissa Hinkle sat in the dusk by the side of the bed. She looked at the ring on her left hand and smiled. Her fiancé had flown in and placed the ring several days before, telling her the delay in receiving it was due to his lengthy search for just the right one.

The large ranch house was buzzing with family and friends. There seemed to be people everywhere. Her husband to be had assured her that it was her turn to sit with the patient, while he visited with and entertained the patient's children upstairs. It had been a long few days, and everyone had pitched in to help this family back to health. She wondered if she would be up to family life. Her confidence surged. Of course she would be. After all, she was a teacher. She had charge of thirteen children in the one room schoolhouse on the Blue River. They ranged in age from second to ninth grade. She had been teaching for the past five years, and had loved every minute of it.

In a few days, however, she would be getting married in front of the fireplace in the living room just down the hall, and although she told Hobbie she would stay on until the board found a replacement or sub, she would give up the teaching for now. She was a bit apprehensive about joining the ranks of the ranch wives on the Blue, even though AC had taught her well about ranch life over the past several weeks. Since the board was still interviewing substitute teachers, Melissa would not have to come under the other wives' scrutiny just yet. Not that the women would not accept her. She had been in the community for five years, but not as a ranch wife.

In the bed before her was the woman AC had said might be interested in having the teaching job. She hoped Lisa would be on her feet soon. Missy had a three-week honeymoon awaiting her, and there was no way she would give up a day of it.

Lisa opened her eyes slowly. "Dustie?"

"No, I'm Melissa, ma'am," She reached for the cup and placed it in Lisa's outstretched hand.

"The bride to be?" Lisa vaguely remembered.

"Why yes. Someone told you all about it?"

"Dustie."

"AC agreed to the wedding in the front room. I just love that fireplace in there, and the whole log house. It's wonderful," Melissa beamed.

Lisa was now well enough to suddenly put things together. The boys talking of Miss Hinkle being at the ranch, AC's comments about Miss Hinkle getting married and the school looking for a teacher, Dustie's talk about the bride to be all made sense to her now. AC and Melissa were going to get married, and the wedding was at the very place she laid wearily in the bedroom, in just a few days! Now it was Lisa's heart that felt sick. She had to get out of there, and back to her home in Alpine. She was trying to recover in the room that would soon belong to Mr. and Mrs. Arlow Greening. She felt suddenly crushed and foolish. She had not made the phone call she had started to make a hundred times since Labor Day, to admit she was wrong. She realized, with Rita's help, that she did love AC, and Grant would want her to do the best for all of them. Hadn't these past few days, the past year and a half been proof that AC was the best for all of them? That, however, was all gone now because of Lisa's pride. She rued her stubbornness and pride. Her body was recuperating, but a new pain gripped her soul. Try as she may, she could not stop the tears, and turned away from the woman who now held AC's heart. She was glad for the darkness of the approaching night. She could not show her devastation to her children or AC and his family. She would have to bear her pain by herself again, alone. The fact that it was of her own making did not make it any easier.

37

AC entered the bedroom at 6:00 PM with a tray of broth, crackers, toast and flat soda. Lisa was already sitting up in the bed. She smoothed the covers in front of her before he set the tray down. AC could not take his eyes off of her. She looked so much better, the color starting to return to her smooth cheeks. He watched her from the chair beside the bed while she ate, smiling beneath his mustache.

His gaze seemed to make her a little uneasy, but she appeared to be hungry, and ate and drank everything on the tray. As AC lifted the tray away he asked, "You feel up to havin' visitors?" His eyes twinkled.

"I believe I do." She smiled back.

AC returned in a moment, with a trail of children behind him. He looked like a duck leading his little ducklings. Lisa's eyes moistened as her children surrounded her and fell upon her with hugs and kisses. If she had been paying attention, she would have seen AC beam with pride beneath his mustache before slipping quietly from the room.

Later that afternoon, everyone gathered in the living room for the Christmas celebration. It didn't matter that it was two days late. They were all healthy, all together, and all very happy.

"Look who I've got," Dustie announced cheerfully, as she led Lisa around the staircase leading to the second floor of the log home, and into the large living area. The children were scattered around the room, and on the couch sat AC,

Melissa Hinkle, and another man whom Lisa had not seen before, although he looked vaguely familiar.

A tall, slender young man rushed to Lisa's other side before AC could rise from the couch. Dustie and the man steadied her, but Lisa felt sick to her stomach, gasped, and clasped her hand to her mouth, not so much as to stop from vomiting, as to stifle a sob. The two swept her back to the bedroom quickly. The minute Lisa hit the bed she broke into sobs. AC and the strange man appeared at her side, as Lisa struggled to control herself. She could not, would not make a scene. Dustie and the young man stood back, concern evident on their faces, but quickly herded everyone else who had followed them, out of the room.

AC knelt beside the bed and collected her hand in his. "Lisa, darlin', this is Doc Hayden. He's been doctoring you and the little ones. Are you feelin' sick again?" He turned, "Here, Doc, take a look." He quickly rose to his feet and moved out of the way, keeping Lisa's hand in his.

Doc Hayden stepped in. His face held a guarded smile, but his eyes were kind and compassionate. He spoke quietly and confidently, "Tell me what's going on, Mrs. Taff, do you feel nausea? Do you have any pain?" He took her wrist as he spoke and looked at his watch.

Lisa did not trust herself to speak. She kept her eyes closed and shook her head.

"Are you feeling weak?"

She nodded.

"Faint?"

Again she nodded.

"Nauseous?"

She nodded again, keeping her eyes closed. She could not, however, keep the tears from seeping through her eyelids.

"Where is your pain?" the doctor gently probed.

"No pain," she finally whispered, "just weak."

"We might've got her up too soon?" AC questioned, "But she seemed so much better just a while ago."

"The fever is gone, " Doc stated, "A cool washcloth for her forehead, again, and quiet rest. We can try again later." He nodded and winked to AC before he left the room.

AC pulled the chair across the room to the edge of the bed again and gently stroked Lisa's face with the washcloth.

Lisa calmed considerably, but tears continued to escape her eyelids.

"Lisa, darlin'…what's the matter? Are you crashing again?" concern was evident in AC's voice, but Lisa could not open her eyes.

"Lisa."

"Don't call me darling, Arlow," she whispered. "Thank you so much for everything, but we need to go home, now." She resolved to open her eyes, and glanced at AC.

AC knelt by the bed, searching her eyes. "You can't go home right now, you are just getting your legs back, and the little ones aren't ready to be taking care of you yet. Surely you know that, Lisa."

"I don't want to be an intrusion on the wedding. We need to go home. I'll call Rita to come over." Lisa had composed herself enough to stop the stream of tears and look into AC's face, hoping to hide her grief.

"The wedding isn't for another four days. The priority here is getting you and your family better."

"Does Melissa share that sentiment?"

"I'm sure she understands. She and Emma have everything pretty much covered."

"She must be one very special woman. Congratulations. You really deserve someone wonderful."

"Huh?"

"You deserve a wonderful wife like Melissa," Lisa croaked between sniffs.

AC cocked his head to one side, sighed, closed his eyes and put his head down on the bed beside her arm. Fresh tears flowed. When AC looked up, one side of his mustache rose slightly as he shook his head.

"I am not marrying Miss Hinkle, Lisa," he said with some amusement in his voice.

"It's OK, Arlow, she told me you have been familiarizing her with the ranch. She told me you were getting married in

140

the living room. I wish you all the best," she was determined to be strong.

"Lisa," he said, the amusement in his voice giving way to slight irritation, "I am not getting married to Melissa Hinkle."

"You're not?"

"No," he stood up and ran his hand through his hair. He turned to her again and began an explanation. "Doc Hayden is marrying Melissa Hinkle. He has a practice in Tucson and flies his little Cessna in here, but not every day. I've been showin' Miss Hinkle the ins and outs of keepin' a ranch runnin' while Doc is back and forth to Tucson. They're my nearest neighbors. Doc and I go way back. I'm just helpin' them out. You do what you can for neighbors out here."

Lisa couldn't believe what she was hearing. Was she happy or sad? She didn't know what she was. Embarrassment rushed through her cheeks. "She said you were getting married in the living room, by the big fireplace she loves, in the house she loves," Lisa said softly.

AC let out a sigh. "She must have said **she** was getting married in my living room. Right now, Doc has a small cabin, but he's working on building a bigger one. It's not quite finished yet, so they're getting hitched at my house. Doc and Missy have been stayin' here at the ranch helpin' with you and the little ones, and helping Emma and Dustie get things all ready for the wedding. It is just easier than driving all around."

"Oh."

"Oh?"

"What else can I say, Arlow, this is like the twilight zone or something. I can't believe I'm so…"

"Jumpy to conclusions?"

"Yes," she smiled at the phrase, "Jumpy to conclusions."

"Well maybe it wasn't too much of a jump with you bein' so feverish and all," he said gruffly.

"I'm sorry, Arlow."

"No time for sorry, let's work on getting you better," he turned to leave, but spun around and sat back down on the edge of the bed, "Anyway, you turned me down, so it wouldn't bother you much if I was getting married, would it?" He wondered if that was too much of a dig, and instantly regretted it.

She looked at him in stunned silence for a moment. He drew her to him and pressed her head and shoulders against his chest.

"Yes, it would," she murmured softly.

38

Later that evening, with a guitar and fiddle playing, they sang, read from the Bible, and at Tom's urging, everyone shared something from the past year or few days that God had done with or for them. The doctor and Melissa Hinkle snuggled on the couch, Emma and Hobbie cuddled on the love seat, the boys spread out on the floor with Dustie and Tom, and Lisa sat in an overstuffed chair by the staircase with Becky in her lap. AC distributed a stack of presents to each person.

"We almost had to make a separate trip for all those presents," Tom teased, "As it was, I had to hold Dustie-girl on my lap in the pilot's seat, and we just piled all those on top of ol' AC!"

Everyone laughed. Squeals of excitement rose as the boys unwrapped western shirts, bandanas, Wranglers, hats, and vests. Becky opened a denim skirt, a shiny pink western blouse, a white rhinestone-studded vest trimmed with fringe, and white boots, also fringed. That she looked cute was an understatement. Lisa slowly unwrapped Wranglers, a denim blouse, and a leather vest with beadwork on each side. Another box contained a denim skirt and red silk western blouse. There was, of course, also a bottle of red nail polish in the stash. When she could finally meet AC's eyes, his smile filled his entire face, spilled over into his eyes, and nearly took up the whole room. "If you all are visiting here for a while, it is about time you get proper clothes for the ranch," he jousted.

"Well, I guess I can finally get out of these pajamas and robe!" she said too shakily, and scurried off to the bedroom. She slumped on the edge of the bed. She was overwhelmed with such deep sorrow, and joy, and who knew what else. Her emotions were at the same time crushing and lifting her. She could not let these people, who had so tenderly and thoroughly cared for her and her children the last week, see her in such a state.

There was a knock on the door, and Dustie's voice called out softly, "Are you OK, honey?" She pushed the door open and came to Lisa's side without being asked, but Lisa was glad she did. "Don't be afraid, girl... just go with it," she looked deep into Lisa's sea green eyes and brushed the hair back from her shoulders. The Lord has gotten you through this far... you know He's not goin' to turn you loose now!" She spoke as if she knew Lisa better than Lisa knew herself.

"AC's got a heart as big as Texas, and pure gold to boot. He was my rock growin' up, until I found Tom." A satisfied smile spread across her soft face, "I think he may be looking for another position now that I have Tom. I don't think he is meaning to pressure you, AC is just a giver, that's all."

She sat on the edge of the bed and looked straight into Lisa's teary eyes. "I know that we seem really different on the outside, Lisa, but underneath we are all pretty much the same, no matter how we talk or look, or what we come from. We're all scared, shell-shocked, and hurtin' in some way ... and very much in need of each other." Her tender gaze penetrated Lisa to the center of her heart. Lisa nodded as if listening to advice from her mother. Dustie gave her a quick hug and headed for the door. She turned to flash her white smile, "Now come on, girl... we're fixin' to have a fashion show!"

144

39

Lisa descended the stairs after tucking her children into bed upstairs. They had been tired and nodded off easily.

AC could feel her enter the room, and turned to see her at the bottom step. His heart skipped a beat. It would be a challenge to his self-control to have her up and around and well in his home. He was at the same time happy and chagrined at the clothes Dustie had helped him pick out for her. The new jeans hugged her just right. He did not remember crossing the large living room to take her in his arms, but she was there, and she filled his arms with sweet warmth and his heart with pure joy.

Lisa had watched him from across the room, tall and strong, his wavy blonde hair slightly tousled. He turned quickly to meet her eyes, and Lisa watched a light creep over him like a wave. His motion was swift and sure as he gathered her into his embrace and found her cheek with a light tease of his mustache. She melted into his embrace. She had felt this before, and the realization that she was ready to feel again eased over her as surely as AC's bold lips. Suddenly she knew it was right.

"Not tonight," he whispered against her shoulder as he labored to pull himself away from their embrace. He was suddenly aware that he had voiced this silent admonition meant for himself. He would not hurt her or their relationship.

He respected her too much to dishonor her. He respected himself enough to not take advantage of her trust in him.

"I may have to sleep in the bunkhouse tonight," he chuckled and held Lisa at arm's length to regain his composure.

"I'm going to sleep upstairs with Becky," Lisa stated resolutely. "There are two beds in her room, and you will have your room back," she flashed a smile, "with my sincere gratitude for your care during my illness," she continued with feigned formality.

"No!" he nearly shouted. The thought of trying to sleep in the bed where she had been was too much. "I mean... eh... you can use my room as a guest room... I mean...I couldn't..."

Lisa ignored AC's outburst and calmly gathered her few things from his room. She reappeared momentarily with the small bundle. "I insist," she smiled softly, spreading AC's entire being with a warm glow. "Your room officially belongs back to the Ranch Boss." She sauntered past him and up the stairs. "Good night," she called behind her.

AC had to sit down. Her charms were potent. Moments later he closed the door a bit too loudly, and crunched through the snow to the bunkhouse.

40

AC rose in the early dawn. He was sure there was no movement in the house yet. He eased quietly into the kitchen where the aroma of freshly brewed coffee in the timer operated coffeemaker filled the air. He headed for the door to his bedroom for a quick shower, when it abruptly opened and Lisa stepped into the shadowy room dressed in the outfit AC had given her. Her appearance startled both of them. They stood speechless facing each other for a moment.

He looked so appealing, his blonde hair sticking out wildly from his hat, stubble of a beard, and the ever-present mustache that Lisa had come to like, not just to tolerate.

As her gaze continued, a hot flush rose in his cheeks. Man, she looked good, and her perfume was just starting to reach his nostrils. He inhaled deeply before he spoke. He knew he had to break the spell or succumb to it.

"Good mornin'," was all he could manage, a faint smile passing across his lips.

"Do you always sneak up on people early in the morning?" she quizzed.

"Not generally... no," he stammered, "I thought you were upstairs."

Now it was Lisa's cheeks that burned. "It was so early... and I figured you were... and this one has a tub," She looked at the tile floor.

AC's laughter rang through the early morning silence.

" The coffee is ready if you're up for some," he finally chuckled. He poured two mugs of the rich dark liquid and handed her one.

"You are a sight." He glanced at her and then down into his mug, "I just might have to kiss those pretty lips... make sure you're awake this mornin'," he kept his gaze on his coffee mug; afraid he was being too bold with her.

"Before coffee?" she asked in mock surprise.

"Before coffee... and after coffee..." AC ventured to raise his eyes to meet Lisa's.

She brought the mug quickly to her lips, but her eyes teased above the rim. "Thank you," she smiled above the cup and sipped again.

"For the coffee, or the offer of a kiss?"

" I think maybe I have been too hasty." She lowered her gaze, avoiding the question.

"Hasty? I don't see you as exactly bein' hasty about anything."

"I think I may have been too hasty in my judgment of you. I'm sorry."

"Aw, don't be sorry, as long as you think I'm OK now."

"I think you are more than OK now. I don't know how I can ever repay you for all you have done for my children and me. You are certainly one of a kind, Mr. Greening."

148

AC cleared his throat suddenly, " I better take my one of a kindness out and do the chores. You make yourself at home, Lisa, whatever you want, you just make yourself at home." He retrieved his hat and headed out the door.

41

Everyone was outside, and after a short nap, Lisa sat curled on the couch, with a hot cup of Emma's peppermint tea, facing the large fireplace. It was large enough for a young child to walk right into, and the hearth was a large cement section adjoining the wood floor of the living room. She sat peacefully taking in the warmth and beauty of the huge log house.

She scanned the walls surrounding the fireplace absently, and gasped slightly as she noticed the picture from her closet, hanging on the left wall. She had put it in Brent's gallery at his urging several months before they went to Phoenix. Brent had put a hefty price tag on the piece, and assured her that due to the nature of the piece, unsigned and his final painting, it would be a treasure. She had spent several anguished weeks before finally making the decision to place it in the gallery. Now she was surprised to find it hanging in a beautiful rustic frame in AC's home. Memories flooded her mind, but her heart remained calm and her eyes mostly dry.

She sat in silence, taking in the painting and its environment. She had not heard the door open or close, but Matthew suddenly slipped onto the couch beside her. She glanced at him and smiled. They sat quietly together for a moment.

"Pretty cool, huh?" Matthew finally broke the silence.

" Yes... pretty cool. How did AC get it?"

"After we got back from Phoenix, he went to the gallery and bought it for me… for us really. He said I could keep it here until I found a home for it. We can keep it here until we are ready to take it home."

"Hmm."

" That was the last painting that Dad ever did. I was there when he took the picture for it. Him and me were going to frame it and put it in the gallery just before Dad died, remember?"

"He and I," Lisa said without thinking. "I remember it well," She breathed deeply.

" AC bought it and framed it himself from some wood he had in the barn. I helped sand the wood and varnish it. Do you think some day we might be able to take it home?"

" I think it is pretty much at home right there."

42

The supper was over, dishes washed, baths taken, and children put to bed. Tom and Dustie retired early to get a good night's sleep before their return to Wyoming in the morning. Hobbie and Emma had just said goodnight and disappeared into their suite off of the entryway on the far side of the living room.

AC moved the large black mesh fireplace grate fence to the side, and added two more logs to the fire. It was pleasantly warm in the spacious living room, and the dry logs crackled as the glowing coals burst into energetic flames.

He returned to the couch and Lisa, sitting a little closer than he had a few minutes ago. He put his arm around her shoulder, and she leaned slightly toward him.

"Thank you," she said softly.

"For what?" he looked at her through a slight smile.

"For doing what I couldn't"

He looked at her in puzzlement.

"I just noticed the painting there on the wall today. Matthew said you bought it for him, and told him he could have it when we are ready."

"I thought it might be helpful."

She rested her head lightly against his shoulder, and he set his cheek against her sweet smelling hair. He pulled her closer, gazing at the lapping flames in the fireplace. The night was quiet except for the sounds of the fire, and ticking of the pendulum clock in the far corner. He bent and whispered in Lisa's ear.

"Don't you reckon it is pretty silly to maintain two separate households... when we are really a family?" He had practiced what to say to her the entire night, and what he had just said was not one of the fancy speeches he had rehearsed. He held her shoulders as she turned to face him, and he knew that even behind his mustache, he could not hide his trembling.

"After pining away for you all the past few weeks in Wyoming, my whole family, even Mama, said I should do this. Dustie and Tom came for moral support. I am going to take their advice, and try this again." AC looked at Lisa with warmth in his eyes, despite his obvious nervousness," I am plain struck silly over you, Lisa... and those kids of yours. I love you." He drew her and planted a hesitant kiss on her quivering lips. Looking her in the eyes, he asked, "Will you marry me, Lisa? Can we just be one big happy family?" He longed to put the ring flopping around in his left shirt pocket on her left hand. "We could have a double weddin' day after tomorrow."

Lisa hugged him tight, but said nothing

He continued, "I can't guarantee that you're the first woman I've ever loved, Lisa, but I can guarantee you are the first and only I will love forever and the first I will ever share my bed with."

"I believe I have already spent some time in your bed, Mr. Greening," she batted her eyes.

AC rubbed his chin thoughtfully. "Yes, ma'am, I reckon you have," his eyes twinkled, "I just want to make sure that the next time... I'm in there with you."

Lisa chuckled and rested her head on his muscular chest.

" I can't ever be Grant," he said slowly, "but I will be the best Arlow I ever could be for you... and for your kids."

"How about our kids," she whispered.

"Can I take that for a yes, then?" He reached into his pocket and offered her the ring in his right palm.

"Yes, Arlow, yes I will marry you, and we will both be the best we can for our kids."

He drew her to another kiss. After a long moment he squeezed her close and set his chin against her head. "That sounds mighty fine, yes ma'am, Mrs. Greening, our kids." He smiled broadly underneath his mustache, as she slipped the ring onto her finger.

Author and speaker, Ann Jenkerson, left Wisconsin 28 years ago, headed for adventure in the great Southwest. A teacher by profession, she has also worked on several cattle ranches in Arizona and New Mexico. She currently lives with her husband and children in the Datil Mountains of New Mexico. She is available to speak to groups of any age and size, and can be reached at HC 61, Box 22, Datil, NM 87821 or jenks@gilanet.com.

Cover illustrator, Suzan McKenzie, is an award-winning western artist and leather crafter; and does day work for several local cattle ranches. For more information about her artwork and custom leather craft, contact her at: Western Doin's, HC 61 Box 3912, Datil, NM 87821.

www.ingramcontent.com/pod-product-compliance
Lightning Source LLC
Chambersburg PA
CBHW051831170626
807CB00003B/1129